"The troubles out there have increased. Suicides, fires, accidents, landslides, and even several murders," Smitty said.

"What else?" There was something more; Carter could feel it now.

"Headhunters. Cannibals. Natives hostile, for some unknown reason, to our being on the island."

Carter looked at him, then turned to Hawk who nodded. "We're not serious, are we?"

NICK CARTER IS IT!

"Nick Carter out-Bonds James Bond."
—Buffalo Evening News

"Nick Carter is America's #1 espionage agent."
—Variety

"Nick Carter is razor-sharp suspense."
—King Features

"Nick Carter is extraordinarily big."
—Bestsellers

"Nick Carter has attracted an army of addicted readers . . . the books are fast, have plenty of action and just the right degree of sex . . . Nick Carter is the American James Bond, suave, sophisticated, a killer with both the ladies and the enemy."
—The New York Times

FROM THE NICK CARTER
KILLMASTER SERIES

NICK CARTER

KILLMASTER

DEATH ISLAND

CHARTER BOOKS, NEW YORK

''Nick Carter'' is a registered trademark of The Condé Nast Publications, Inc., registered in the United States Patent Office.

DEATH ISLAND

A Charter Book/published by arrangement with
The Condé Nast Publications, Inc.

PRINTING HISTORY
Charter Original/May 1984

ISBN: 0-441-14220-6

Charter Books are published by The Berkley Publishing Group,
200 Madison Avenue, New York, N.Y. 10016
PRINTED IN THE UNITED STATES OF AMERICA

*Dedicated to the men of the
Secret Service of the United
States of America*

DEATH ISLAND

PROLOGUE

Handley Duvall stepped outside from the Barbarossa Hotel on the South Pacific island of Hiva Faui and squinted up at the tropical sun as he mopped his brow with his handkerchief. This certainly wasn't Boston. It was at least a hundred degrees in the shade, with a humidity that nearly matched.

The electricity had gone out again in the downtown section of the capital city, something that happened at least twice a week, so even in the hotel barroom there had been little or no relief.

Duvall had been promoted last month to mid-shift foreman, which gave him the privilege of hotfooting it into town once a week for the ''booze and treat'' run. Booze for his shift for the week, and the treat was a visit to Madame Leone's, next door to the hotel.

This afternoon he wondered, however, if either was worth a damn. The booze was watered down and overpriced, and without air conditioning the girls at Madame Leone's would be somewhat less than appealing.

His stomach growled, a sharp wave of heartburn rising up at the back of his throat.

''Christ,'' he swore. He hated this place.

He started next door, when he happened to look across the street to the government-run liquor store. Yun Lo, the Chinese shift boy from the site who had come into town to help Duvall, was loading the five cases of booze into the jeep. Only there were several Chinese standing around him. He was passing out bottles of the booze to his friends in exchange for other bottles that he put into the cases, which he then loaded into the jeep.

The goddamned kid is cheating me, Duvall thought. The booze was watered down, all right, but not by the liquor store. It was being done by Yun Lo and probably by all the other Chinese who worked at the receiver site as well.

Duvall, a large man who was over six feet tall and weighed at least two hundred pounds, could feel his blood pressure rising as he hitched up his khakis and charged across the street, the sweat pouring off him, his muscles flexing.

"Hey, you son of a bitch!" he shouted.

Yun Lo and the other Chinese looked up, startled, as did a half-dozen other pedestrians nearby.

One of the Chinese—it looked to Duvall like a woman—dropped the bottle she had been holding, and it shattered on the sidewalk as she sprinted down the street.

The others scattered as well, except for Yun Lo. He stood next to the jeep, smiling uncertainly and bowing repeatedly.

Duvall smashed his fist into the man's left shoulder, sending him skidding up against the jeep.

"You bastard! You son of a bitch!" Duvall screamed, charging after Yun Lo, who stepped aside.

Suddenly Duvall was upside down, and then he was lying on his back on the sidewalk, his head throbbing where he had hit it.

"What the hell . . . ?" he began, and he looked up

into Yun Lo's eyes. The young man was no longer smiling. He stood in a half crouch, his eyes flashing, his teeth bared.

For just an instant something in the back of his mind told Duvall to watch himself, to hold back. Hell, he had been an All-Star halfback at Iowa State. But he was damned mad. He had another eighteen months of this place . . . another year and a half of pure, unadulterated crap to put up with, and already he was sick and tired of it all.

He scrambled to his feet and charged the slightly built Oriental again, swinging as he came. Something very sharp and almost hot pierced his side, causing him to pull back and to the left.

There was no one out on the street now. Half a block away from them was the town square and the police station. Up the hill was the governor's mansion. But they were alone here.

Duvall stood staring stupidly at Yun Lo. The Chinese man held a long, wicked-looking knife from which blood was dripping all the way to the haft.

"You stupid bastard . . ." Duvall said.

Yun Lo turned and unhurriedly walked away. The knife clattered into the gutter as he disappeared around the corner, and a weakness descended over the American, who looked down at the great gash in his side from which his own blood was pumping.

He had been stabbed. Yun Lo had actually stabbed him. *Christ! This is ridiculous! Electrical engineers don't get stabbed on obscure islands in the South Pacific.* Professor Albertson never told him anything like that at Iowa State.

Duvall staggered sideways to the jeep, then shuffled around to the driver's side and managed to climb up behind the wheel. He held his left hand firmly against the wide wound.

Apply direct pressure. Wasn't that what his high

school Red Cross first aid instructor had told them to do?

Somehow he managed to dig out his keys and get the jeep started. He never thought about the hospital around the corner as he pulled away from the curb and accelerated jerkily through town, going out to the sea-coast highway that led fifteen miles to the other side of the island where the Hiva Faui Satellite Tracking and Receiving Station was located.

He passed a couple of trucks on the way out, and a lot of pedestrian traffic heading out to the copra drying pits and presses. But the farther he went, the weaker he became, so that after a while he was having a lot of trouble keeping the jeep on the narrow blacktopped road.

He had been stabbed. Even now it was almost impossible to believe.

Blood was leaking between his fingers, down the side of his hip and leg, but the bleeding had definitely slowed down.

Duvall glanced at the wound, and the jeep suddenly swerved to the right. At the last moment he looked up as the jeep crashed through a thick tangle of brush in the ditch beside the road and crashed into a young palm tree.

For what seemed like an eternity, the American sat in the jeep, his head against the steering wheel, his entire world going round and round. It was as bad as being drunk, the fleeting thought crossed his mind.

After a time he looked up. He was in the middle of a goddamned jungle.

Duvall tried to think. He remembered passing the main copra processing sheds, and then he had safely negotiated the hairpin turns around the cliffs. It meant he was not too far from the site. Perhaps a mile or two at the most.

He pushed open the door and stumbled out, then

pulled his way to the back of the jeep. He could see the road about ten feet above him. It seemed like a thousand feet.

He started up but fell back against the jeep, his right arm flopping against the cases of booze. He looked back, then opened one of the cases, pulled out a bottle, and opened it. He tipped it up and took a deep drink. Immediately he spat it out. It had been watered down. Probably with tea and iodine. The tea for color, the iodine for bite.

He threw the bottle aside and opened a second, this one from a back row. He took a cautious drink. It was whiskey. He took another deep drink, his head spinning around for a second or two, and then he started back up toward the road.

Twice he stumbled and fell back in great pain. Each time, he took another deep drink, then started up, finally reaching the road as the tropical sun began to go down and the voracious mosquitoes came out.

Immediately he started up the gentle incline, staggering from one side of the road to the other.

Once he thought he heard a siren sounding from above, and he stopped and held his breath. But the wind was blowing up from the sea, and after a while he started up again, not at all sure he had heard anything.

It was fully dark when he came around the last bend in the access road, in full view of the radomes and the four huge satellite tracking dishes. He was numb by now, his head buzzing. He had long since discarded the whiskey bottle, most of its contents gone. But he knew that what he was seeing was all wrong. Terribly wrong.

There were fires everywhere throughout the tracking site, and now he could definitely hear sirens, and something else . . . gunfire. He was sure it was gunfire!

"Jesus . . ." he swore out loud, his voice hoarse,

and he redoubled his efforts, hobbling up the road.

As he got closer he could definitely hear gunshots, and he could hear people shouting and screaming.

The site was under attack. But by whom? It didn't make sense. Nothing that had happened that day made any sense to Duvall.

The main gate was lying half off its hinges, the odor of cordite very strong, but the gunshots and cries finally ended. The siren, however, kept on wailing as Duvall cautiously approached.

There were several bodies lying on the blacktop. Some of them were dark-skinned and clothed only in loincloths. But two of them, sprawled near the guardhouse, wore khaki uniforms.

Duvall hurried over to those bodies and turned one of them over.

Christ! It was Wolchek! They had played poker together in the group last night.

Duvall looked up. What had happened here? What in God's name had happened?

He picked up Wolchek's .45 automatic, awkwardly checked to make sure there was a round in the chamber, and he cocked the hammer back and entered the tracking site. Suddenly the alarm cut off and he froze.

The silence was eerie. There were several bodies on the road ahead of him and a burned-out truck. Smoke rose from a building farther up the hill, but the dishes and radomes seemed intact.

Someone came running down the hill from Administration, and Duvall swiveled around, bringing up the .45. But he realized it was one of the technicians. Then his knees gave way beneath him.

What is going on, he thought as he fell to the roadway. *What in hell is happening here . . . ?*

ONE

The azure sky out to sea seemed to merge with the fairy-tale blue of the Mediterranean as the yacht *Marybelle* worked her way northeast up the coast of France from Cannes to her winter berth at Monaco.

It was still early, before noon, as Nick Carter, clad in bathing trunks and a short terrycloth robe, emerged onto the afterdeck where the stewards had laid out champagne and breakfast.

"Good morning, Monsieur Carter," Henri-Rieves, the assistant chief steward said, holding out Carter's chair.

"It is a good morning, isn't it," Carter said, breathing deeply, drinking in the sweetly scented sea air. "When are we due at Monaco?"

"Not until after lunch, *monsieur*. Mademoiselle Gordon instructed that we stop for an hour or two off Antibes."

"Another wreck?"

"Perhaps more Roman amphorae, *monsieur*."

"Perhaps," Carter said. The steward poured him a glass of crackling cold Dom Perignon, served him a bit of beluga, some toast, and shirred eggs, then retired gracefully belowdecks.

The gentle motion of the ship easing its way through calm seas, the fine, well-chilled wine, and the comfortable surroundings were deeply relaxing at that moment. Carter sighed deeply. It had been years since he had had a vacation half so purely restful as this one had been.

For the past two weeks he had been cruising the French Riviera aboard the *Marybelle*, a 210-foot yacht owned by Lady Pamela Gordon, the thirty-year-old daughter of Sir Donald Gordon, former MP and chief of the SIS back in the late fifties and early sixties. Sir Donald and David Hawk, Carter's boss and head of the United States's supersecret intelligence agency, AXE, were old friends, going back together before World War II. It was only natural that Carter had been introduced to Lady Gordon, and last month the invitation to join her for the beginning of her fall-winter cruise had come.

He had another ten days before he had to report to the AXE Rehab and Retraining Facility in Arizona, and his plans included Lady Gordon's villa in Monaco and a bit of baccarat in Monte Carlo.

"Two weeks, and you're already going soft on me," a mellifluous woman's voice came from behind him.

Carter turned around as Lady Gordon, her deep, rich tan stunning against her almost nonexistent yellow bikini, came on deck. She was frowning.

"Enough clay pots, Pamela," Carter said, laughing. "I'm on vacation."

She came around and kissed him on the cheek, then took her place across the small table from him. Henri-Rieves glided to her elbow, the champagne bottle in hand.

"*Mademoiselle*," he said.

"Please," she said, looking into Carter's eyes.

The steward poured her wine and brought her a

lightly salted musk melon half with a bit of cream and a few strawberries on the side, then left.

"Didn't you sleep?" she asked, sipping her wine.

"Like a log."

"Why were you up so early, then?"

"You've done well for the last two weeks. Don't try to arrange my next ten days," Carter said. Lady Gordon's problem had been—and always would be, he suspected—that she did not feel comfortable unless she had arranged the lives of everyone around her. She was a natural-born organizer. Everyone in London—and half of the regulars on the French, Spanish, and Italian Rivieras—was trying to marry her off to a diplomat. She would make a perfect consul's wife or the consort of an ambassador somewhere.

"Sorry, Nicholas," she said, turning her head. "I hope you don't mind that we're stopping at the twelve-foot ledge off Antibes."

"Not at all . . ." Carter started to say, when Henri-Rieves came up. He was carrying a telephone.

"Pardon, monsieur," he said. "There is a call for you." He plugged the telephone in the afterdeck panel and set the instrument on the table in front of Carter, who picked it up.

"Carter here."

"Mr. Carter, I'm so happy I was able to reach you," an excited man's voice came over the line. This was trouble, Carter sensed.

"What can I do for you?"

"Pardon me. I'm Roger Morton, chargé d'affaires for the United States embassy in Paris, and I have a message for you, sir."

"This is an open line, Morton," Carter said. He was looking at Pamela, who was pouting. She sensed it meant trouble as well.

"Ah . . . yes, sir, I understand that. I merely telephoned to pass a message, sir."

"Go ahead. I'll take your message."

"This is from Amalgamated Press. You are to return home immediately. There is an important assignment for you. End of message, sir."

Pamela had gotten up, and she came around the table to Carter and leaned over him, running her fingers through the hairs on his chest as she nibbled on his left ear.

"Who was the signatory?"

"D.W. Hawkins."

It was David Hawk. "All right, Morton. Thank you for your help."

"Any reply, sir?" the chargé hastened to ask.

"None. Thanks again," Carter said. As he put down the phone, Pamela straightened up, smiled provocatively, and sauntered back into the main salon and into the owner's stateroom.

Carter smiled. He drank the rest of his champagne, then got up and went up the ladder to the fly deck and up the second ladder to the bridge. Captain Phillipe Jourdain, his dress whites immaculate, looked up when Carter entered.

"Ah, Monsieur Carter, how may I be of assistance this morning?"

"I need to get to Nice as quickly as possible, Captain. I have a plane to catch."

"I am so very sorry, *monsieur*, but Mademoiselle Gordon has issued us our instructions . . ."

Carter reached out and picked up the phone, then punched the numbers for the owner's stateroom. He switched to intercom.

"Pamela, this is Nicholas. I've told your captain to make for Nice."

"Yes, Nicholas," Pamela said, her voice husky. "But am I to be kept waiting here all morning?"

"No," Carter said, eyeing the embarrassed captain. He put down the telephone. "What is our ETA?"

"It will take us two hours at full speed, Monsieur Carter," the captain said.

"Get me to the public docks, then I'll need a taxi to the airport," Carter said, and he turned and went below.

Pamela was waiting for him, nude on the king-size bed in the owner's stateroom. They had been going on like this for two weeks, but now Carter was almost glad that Hawk had called him away. He was beginning to feel just a bit *kept*.

Carter had no problems getting a seat on the 2:00 P.M. flight to Paris from Nice, and from there the evening TWA flight into Washington's National Airport.

Pamela had put up a fuss at the docks, however, insisting that she come along with him and straighten out his boss about his vacation time. She had even been willing to place a call to the President.

Carter had calmed her down, promised to rejoin her as soon as he could, and to placate her, he even left his tuxedo aboard.

"Hurry back, Nicholas," she breathed into his ear. "We'll have a marvelous fall together. You'll see. I will have everything arranged by the time you return."

He disengaged himself from her, they kissed once again, and he took a cab. By the time he had rounded the corner from the quay, the *Marybelle* was already pulling out. Pamela wasted no time.

A chill wind blew off the Potomac as Nick Carter retrieved his bags, hurried through customs, and went outside to look for a cab. It was just a few minutes after midnight, Washington time, but his body clock told him it was six hours later. He was dead tired.

Tom LaMotta, one of AXE's staff drivers, was waiting for him just ahead of the taxi stands. There was a lot of traffic from the late-night Paris arrival.

"Mr. Carter," a familiar voice called out, and Carter looked around tiredly as the round, cheerful driver came across and plucked both suitcases out of his hands.

"Didn't expect to see you here, Tom," Carter said, following the driver back to the nondescript Chevy.

"We knew you were coming in on the midnight TWA."

"Just get me home. I'm beat."

LaMotta opened the trunk and tossed Carter's bags inside. "Sorry about that, sir, but the brass is waiting for you."

Carter was instantly awake, the adrenaline suddenly pumping. "Is Smitty there?" he asked. Rupert Smith was AXE's new head of Operations. If he was waiting, something immediate was happening.

"Yes, sir," LaMotta said.

They drove north past the Pentagon to the Key Bridge, and once across the river they cut back on M Street to New Hampshire, which they took up to Dupont Circle where AXE maintained its headquarters under the cover of Amalgamated Press and Wire Services.

LaMotta parked in the basement garage and took care of the luggage while Carter signed in and went directly up to Operations on the fourth floor. He had to be signed in again by security there, then had to punch the six-digit code for the access door.

LaMotta had called ahead. Rupert Smith was waiting for him, a thick bundle of file folders before him. He did not look pleased.

"Sorry to have to cut your vacation short like this, Carter," Smith said. He was very tall and very thin, almost skeletal-looking. He had served in various capacities in the Central Intelligence Agency for the past fifteen years, but when the Company had become too tame for him, he had transferred to AXE. He was very good at his job.

One of his people stuck his head in the door. "He's ready, sir. Will you be needing Karsten?"

"Is he ready?"

"Yes, sir."

"Very good. I want you down in Archives. We may have some more cross-referencing to tidy up the loose ends yet tonight."

"Yes, sir."

Smith, who had been seated behind his desk, got up and came around. Carter got to his feet.

"No rest for the wicked, I'm afraid," Smith said. "But David wants to see you."

"Hawk is here? Tonight?"

Smith nodded. "I don't know the source, but he's taken this as one of his pet projects. It's why you were called, of course."

They went out into the corridor and started toward the private elevator, which was the only access up to executive territory on the fifth floor.

"Something's happened somewhere?" Carter asked. When he had left for vacation with Pamela, everything here had seemed to be on a fairly even keel. No trouble spots had been developing as far as he knew. He said as much to Smith.

"This has been hatching for the past year or two, from what I gather," Smith said. "But NASA was handling it until two months ago, until the Navy took over security."

Carter was about to ask "Security for what?" when Herb Karsten, the major domo of facts, figures, and instant references for AXE, stepped out of his office and joined them.

"Nick," he said, extending his hand. "Trust you had a good vacation?"

"Not bad. Been here long?"

"All night."

They took the elevator up, their passes were checked, and they strode down the corridor into Hawk's outer office. His secretary, Ginger Bateman, was gone, but the inner door was open, and Smith led them through.

David Hawk was a short, very stocky man with a thick shock of white hair and a short bulldoglike neck. He was smoking a dreadful cigar as usual, and he took it out of his mouth and looked up as they came in.

"Are you fit, Nick?" he grumbled without preamble.

Smith closed the door behind them.

"Yes, sir," Carter said.

"You were scheduled for retraining and testing this quarter. Are you ready for an assignment without it?"

"I think I can manage, sir," Carter said. He, no less than anyone else in AXE, had a very deep and abiding respect for David Hawk, the chief. What Hawk said, went. He was hardly ever wrong. And no one, absolutely *no* one, ever lied to him, or over- or underestimated any situation. When he asked a question, he expected an absolutely honest, totally straight answer.

"Have a seat, then, gentlemen. We have a lot of ground to cover tonight," Hawk said.

They all took seats across from Hawk. Smith opened his top file folder and thumbed through the papers it contained. Karsten sat back.

"What do you know about the Caroline Islands?" Hawk began.

"A group in the Pacific . . . north of the equator, I think. South of Japan. U.S. trust territory. Truk is there and Hall Island and maybe Bikini."

"Correct on all but Bikini . . . it's in the Marshall Islands. Nearby. But you understand that not much happens out there these days."

"Satellite tracking and receiving stations?" Carter asked.

"That's the extent of it," Hawk said, glancing at Smith. "Which is exactly our problem."

Smith took up the briefing. "The Faui Faui island group within the Carolines," he began. "Have you heard of them?"

Carter admitted he had not.

"Five inhabited islands, plus numerous other coral atolls. Faui Faui itself—which is one of the smaller islands—then Tamau Faui, Akau Faui, Natu Faui—where the biggest native population lives—and then Hiva Faui. Hiva Faui is the main island and on it is the capital city of the same name."

"In the Carolines?"

"Yes. Just east of Hall, northeast of Truk, and almost directly north of Oroluk. Lots of white sand beaches, hot days and warm evenings, volcanoes, natives, all that sort of thing."

"But curiously enough, the French actually own it all," Karsten put in.

Carter looked toward him. "I thought it was all a U.S. trust."

"All but the Faui Faui group. Much of that area was French before the war, and then after we liberated it all from the Japanese we took it over. All but the Faui Faui group. There were apparently a number of French families who sacrificed a lot during the war. De Gaulle insisted, and the group remained in French control."

"But with a rather important treaty, as it turns out," Smith added.

"French cooperation," Carter said.

"Yes. Much like Guantánamo Bay. Despite the French histrionics of the sixties and seventies, we managed to hang on to our bit of land on Hiva Faui."

"Satellite tracking?" Carter asked.

"Yes," Smith replied.

"Spy-in-the-Sky satellite," Hawk said. "Inter-agency. Big stuff."

"I see," Carter said. "How long have we had this operation running?"

"In one form or another since the mid-sixties," Smith said. "Actually, it was one of our first. We watch the Far East from there. Before that it was routine electronic surveillance. Radio and cryptography, and things like that."

"I get the picture," Carter said. "So what's happening out there now that has us worried? Sabotage? A mole?"

"That's just it," Smith said. "We really don't know."

"But it has to stop," Karsten added.

Smith thumbed deeper into the files he held on his lap. He looked up at Hawk, who nodded for him to go on, then cleared his throat.

"In January 1969, Tom Hawkins, a technician at what was then called Number 17HF Site, apparently committed suicide. They found him hanging in the forest," Smith said. He paused just a moment and went on. "August 1971, Stew Scharaga, Donald Deutsch, and Wally Hoggins died when the truck they were driving apparently went out of control and crashed over a cliff just down from the station. May '74, and again in July of '75, '76, and '78, there were major fires at the station. A total of fourteen people killed, twenty-seven injured."

"The list goes on?" Carter asked. He had a funny feeling about what he was being told, although he had no idea where it was going.

"Indeed," Smith said. "The troubles out there increased. Suicides, fires, accidents, landslides, and even several murders."

"What else?" There was something more; Carter could feel it now.

"Headhunters. Cannibals. Natives hostile, for some reason, to our being on the island."

Carter looked at him, then turned to Hawk who nodded. "We're not serious, are we?"

"Perfectly," Smith said. "In the last five and a half years there have been seventeen technicians killed, another thirty or so wounded. And that's not counting the various cases of physical and mental exhaustion reporting back from Hiva Faui."

"What have we done about it?" Carter asked. He could not believe he was hearing what he was.

"As far as the accidents, suicides, and fights among the staff go, not a lot," Smith said. "As far as the attacks go, we've cleaned out Natu Faui and Akau Faui at least three times. Or at least the Navy has."

"To no effect?"

"Apparently not," Hawk said, sitting forward. "It's technically a French protectorate. There isn't a whole lot we can do about it."

"Surely security is—"

"Security is and always has been very good at the Hiva Faui site," Hawk said. "Somehow, though, the natives always find a way of getting through."

Carter sat back and lit one of his cigarettes that were specially made for him in a small shop in Washington. The paper was black, and his initials were stamped in gold near the tip. The tobacco was very strong.

"I'm to go out there and see what the trouble is."

"Something like that, Nick," Hawk said. "You're to see a Justin Owen—he's the station manager—and a Handley Duvall who witnessed a part of the last native attack."

"I see, sir," Carter said. "Who's in charge of the island? I mean, who is the French governor, or isn't there such a position?"

"Indeed there is," Smith said. "Albert Remi Rondine. He and his family own an enormous amount of stock in French manufacturing . . . especially steel and oil.''

"Yet he chooses to be governor of a tiny Pacific island group?'' Carter asked.

"He is quite a colorful character, actually,'' Karsten said. "He was born in Hong Kong in 1930 or '31, and when the war broke out he was taken prisoner by the Japanese.''

"How'd he end up on Hiva Faui?''

"We don't know. But he is autocratic. He hates Americans. And he has a wife and at least half a dozen mistresses. It's his little kingdom.''

"You want me to find out what or who is killing our people and put a stop to it on Hiva Faui.''

"Exactly,'' Hawk said.

"Our people at the tracking station call it Death Island,'' Karsten added.

TWO

Heading west, San Francisco was very nice for a night's stay, and Honolulu was expensive and very cosmopolitan. But after that things began to get a bit primitive by comparison. At Wake Island, the local BOQ—which the soldiers stationed there jokingly called the Holiday Inn—was a two-story barracks that had been built during World War II and had seen very few improvements since then, but there was hot water, and every room had its own shower and sink. At Agaña, on Guam, no one had the guts to call the accommodations anything but the "crash pad." And by the time the Faui Faui group showed up as a number of thick clouds on the horizon from the cockpit of an ancient but still serviceable DC-3, Carter had to wonder if he hadn't slipped backward in time.

They were bringing supplies down from Hall Island for the Hiva Faui Satellite Tracking and Receiving Station, and Tim Torrence, the sardonic civilian pilot, had nothing good to say about the place.

"The French may own it, and the Americans may work there, but the Chinese run the joint," the man said.

They had already begun their long descent, and the

copilot, a little man from New Zealand, was just waking up. The cockpit smelled like a cross between lubricating oil and body odor. It was not very pleasant.

"What do you mean?" Carter asked. "I would have thought the Japanese would be here, if there were any Orientals."

Torrence laughed out loud. "You've got a lot to learn if you think anything like that, pal. The Japanese may have been here for the duration of the war, but right afterward they were either all killed or they hotfooted it back to their home islands."

"The Japanese aren't very well liked here? Still?"

"Still. But neither are the Chinese, for that matter, although the bastards are a fact of life."

They broke out of the intense cloud cover over the main island a few miles north of the end of the runway. Carter sat forward as they came in, and he got a good view of the sprawling satellite receiving station and the radar domes, four of them stark white in contrast to the dark green of the surrounding jungle. But even from here Carter could see where repairs were being made to a long, low brick building, and he could see that a number of the barrackslike structures were blackened by fire.

He swiveled around in his seat and looked toward the south, in the direction of a paved highway. "Where does the road lead?" he asked.

Odets, the copilot, glanced sleepily that way. "Town," he mumbled, and he turned back to the landing.

Torrence was very good. The DC-3 greased in for a landing on the paved runway, and soon they were pulling up and swinging around in front of a long, low building. The engines were cut, and Torrence looked around and grinned. "Here we are, pal, home sweet home. For you, that is."

Carter unstrapped from his seat and worked his way

back to the cargo bay. Odets came back a moment later, undogged the main hatch, and shoved it open. The furnacelike heat hit them in a big rush at the same moment as a canvas-covered truck backed up to the open hatch. There were several men, all dressed in khaki, waiting below.

Carter jumped down, and Odets tossed down his two leather bags. A short, slightly built Chinese man scurried around the truck and scooped up Carter's bags, then hurried over to a jeep with them as a tall, rugged-looking man with red hair came over. Just behind him was an even taller, more heavyset man.

"Nick Carter?" the first man asked, extending his hand. Carter took it.

"Justin Owen?"

"That's right," the red-haired man replied. "I'm station manager out here, although these days that's nothing to brag about." He half turned as the other man came up. It seemed as if he were in pain. "I'd like you to meet my chief engineer, Handley Duvall."

Carter shook hands with him. "How are you feeling, Mr. Duvall? I understand you were wounded in the latest attack."

"No, sir. It was in town . . . one of our civilian workers," Duvall said. It seemed as if he were at his wit's end.

"One of the subcontractors," Owen put in.

"That little s.o.b.," Duvall began, but he became silent at a glance from Owen.

"We have a room set up for you," the station manager said, leading Carter around the truck and over to a second jeep. The Chinese man who had taken Carter's luggage was already gone. Several other Orientals, all dressed in white shorts, white long-sleeved shirts, and straw hats, had begun to unload the aircraft.

Carter looked back. Odets and Torrence stood in the

cargo hatch, and the pilot waved. "See you next month," he shouted.

Carter waved back. "Only one plane a month?" he asked Owen.

" 'Fraid so, Mr. Carter. But even at that, I wouldn't be too optimistic about my chances of being on it. This is a tougher problem than you might think."

"There've been other investigators out here?"

"Investigators, committees, platoons, submarines. The entire gamut. But I'll tell you all about it later. I imagine you'll want to freshen up first, and I'll have the cook rustle you up something to eat."

"Sounds good," Carter said. As he climbed into the jeep with Owen and Duvall, he glanced again back at the plane. Several of the Orientals who were unloading the cargo were looking back. It struck Carter as odd, but then so did Owen and Duvall strike him as odd.

Carter was shown to a room on the second floor of a long wooden building that apparently served as a combination VIP quarters and administrative center. It was across a narrow road from one of the receiving equipment units and just next door to the dining hall. It was small but pleasantly furnished, and most importantly, it was air conditioned. He had his own private bathroom.

His suitcases had already been brought up, and most of his clothing had been unpacked and was hanging in the small closet.

Carter got undressed, took a quick, cool shower, and then got dressed in a pair of lightweight slacks, a military-cut shirt-jacket, and soft slip-on boots. He lit a cigarette as he strapped on Wilhelmina, his Luger, at his belt beneath his shirt, and made sure Hugo, his razor-sharp stiletto, was secure in its chamois sheath at his left ankle. He normally carried it on his forearm, but his shirt was short-sleeved. He also carried a very small gas bomb attached high on his inner thigh, much like a third testicle.

For a time he stared out the window at the activity down in the compound. Duvall had been the one who had been wounded in town by one of the Chinese from the station. From what Carter understood, there was not much love lost between the civilian employees— most of them Oriental—and the station engineers and technicians. But as far as he knew, Duvall's was the first incident stemming from that animosity.

From everything he had been briefed on, there was no connection between what had happened to Duvall and the attacks on the camp. And yet now that he was here, he had to wonder. . . .

Someone knocked at his door, and he turned around as a young Chinese man came in and smiled. "It is time, Mr. Carter. Mr. Owen say your dinner is ready across the way at the club."

"Where is that?" Carter asked, looking closely at the man. It was hard to tell his age or his specific nationality. Taiwanese, possibly, he thought.

"Behind the dining hall, venerable sir."

"Thanks," Carter said, smiling. He stubbed out his cigarette in the ashtray on his desk, then left the room.

After being in the air conditioning, even for just a short time, the temperature and humidity outside were nearly unbearable. He was sweating heavily by the time he made it across to the dining hall. A young man in white coveralls directed him around back to the club. Inside, Owen, Duvall, and a third, thin, sullen-looking man with a military crewcut were waiting for him at a large round table.

Owen waved him over. "You look a little less frazzled than before," he said pleasantly.

Carter sat down, and Owen introduced him to the thin man who, Carter noticed, wore a .357 magnum revolver strapped to his hip.

"Richard Fenster, chief of station security."

Carter nodded, but the man made no move to shake hands. Carter decided he didn't like him. He seemed shifty; his eyes refused to remain on one object for more than an instant.

An Oriental came from behind the bar and laid out several plates of sliced corned beef, thickly sliced rye bread, and all the trimmings, plus a round of cold beers.

"How long have you been out here, Mr. Fenster?" Carter asked, making himself a sandwich.

"Too long. And I don't mind telling you that I resent interference."

"What interference is that?" Carter asked, looking up.

"I've been doing my job out here. I could use more men, not some hot shot investigator from Washington."

"Yes?" Carter said, smiling. He was certain now that he did not like this man.

"We're being counterproductive here . . ." Owen started, but Duvall leaned forward.

"I just want to know how and when you're going to do something about what is happening here." He looked toward the door. "For Christ's sake, we're sitting ducks out here."

"Who attacked the base this time around?" Carter asked the station manager.

"Natives from Natu Faui, we're assuming."

"You're assuming that they were natives, or about their origin?" Carter asked.

"They were natives, all right. But we're assuming they came from Natu Faui."

"That's the island our Navy has cleaned out a few times already?"

Fenster smiled faintly. "Invasions, they called

them, although that would hardly have been my choice of words. More like shore missions, and not very extensive at that. A couple of the patrols were sent inland, and interpreters spoke with the native government.''

''And?'' Carter prompted after a moment or two of silence.

Fenster shrugged. ''Our people were assured each time that the attacks, if they had been mounted from Natu Faui, were the work of a few youngsters who had gotten drunk on whiskey.''

''I see,'' Carter said. ''Where do they get their whiskey?''

Fenster curled his lip. ''The French . . . we believe.''

''Our problems are not isolated to native attacks,'' Owen interjected.

Carter turned to him.

''There have been plenty of other incidents in the past. Including the attack on Handley in town by his section aide.''

''A Chinese man?''

''Yun Lo.'' Duvall spat out the name.

''Is the man in custody?''

Owen shook his head. ''We can't find him. The French have their people out looking for him, of course, since it happened in town. But neither their people nor Fenster's have come up with a clue.''

''Nor will we ever,'' the security chief said. ''Yun Lo has disappeared into the bush like the others. He's living back up there in the hills with his wife and mother and father and grandparents and probably a dozen kids and as many mistresses. They've got it made here. They own these islands.''

'' 'Others'?'' Carter asked.

Owen sighed deeply. ''We have had a problem with

our help out here. They steal things, then disappear. But until the attack on Handley, we felt they were no serious threat to us.''

''You don't believe they have anything to do with your ongoing problem?''

''Not with the attacks on the base,'' Owen said. ''They may be a pain in the ass, but they aren't . . . weren't dangerous.''

''Where are they recruited?''

''Here on the island. There's a fairly extensive population of Orientals.''

''I thought the Japanese—'' Carter started, but Owen cut him off.

''This was a POW camp during the war. A lot of the prisoners from Manchuria and then later from Hong Kong were brought down here. Men, women, children.''

''The Japanese were driven out and the Chinese remained.''

''Exactly.''

''If you're having so much trouble with them why don't you hire your subcontract people from the States?''

''Too expensive.''

''I see.''

Carter ate his excellent lunch as Owen briefly went over the history of the satellite receiving station's troubles. He added nothing new to what Carter had already learned from AXE records. But sitting there now at the station, he felt a sense of continuity with the story that he had not picked up back in Washington. He got the sense that the troubles here over the years had been caused by one group for a specific purpose. He also got the feeling that their troubles had picked up in frequency and intensity during the past year or so. He voiced that opinion to Owen.

''You're damned right it's been getting worse.

Much worse," the station manager said.

"Why?" Carter asked.

Owen was nonplussed for just a moment. He looked to Fenster. Then back. "It beats the hell out of me, Carter. I don't know."

"Has anything different been happening with operations over the past year or two? Any new intelligence seam? New equipment?"

Owen suddenly seemed uncomfortable. "Yes to all counts, but it's not something I'd care to discuss here in the open."

"I'm finished with my lunch," Carter said, getting up.

"We can go to my office, then."

The four men left the club and went back across the street and into the administration building. Owen's office was near the back of the building, large, carpeted, and air conditioned. A large window looked out over the fenced area that contained the shortwave and some of the microwave antennae for communications with various ships and planes throughout the Pacific and Far East.

At the door Duvall excused himself, saying he had to return to work. "I hope you will finally put a stop to this, Mr. Carter," he said. Then he left.

"Handley is having a hard time of it here, I'm afraid," Owen said as they entered his office and took seats.

"Because of the attack?"

"That too, but he's not fit in since the day he arrived. He counts the days until his contract is up."

"You've offered him the option of quitting?"

Owen nodded. "He says he needs the money and the reference."

Carter turned suddenly to Fenster. "How long have you been here?"

"Entirely too long," the man shot back darkly.

Carter waited.

"Thirty-two months," the man finally said. "I renewed my contract for an additional two years."

Carter managed a faint smile as he turned back to Owen. "I was asking about your operations over the past year or two."

"Yes," Owen said. "About two and a half years ago, as you may or may not know, we put up a new stationary-orbit satellite over the China Sea to keep watch on China as well as Vietnam, Cambodia, and Laos. The entire region. At the same time that system was being put into operation, we were installing new receiving equipment and new photographic analysis gear. State of the art."

"Have we picked up anything from it?"

Owen nodded. "The quality of our intelligence report has risen significantly."

Carter's eyes narrowed. "Do you have intelligence evaluators and analysts out here?"

"No," Owen said. "But from the raw data that we relay back to D.C., it's been very easy to see what the Spy-in-the-Sky system has been doing for us."

Carter glanced toward the window. The day *looked* hot. "Is there a connection between our successes with Chinese intelligence and the fact that your subcontractors here are all ethnic Chinese?"

Fenster broke in at that. "That was the first thing everyone thought, Mr. Carter. And for my time here I've looked into every rumor, chased down every lead, and tried to figure every angle."

"Nothing?"

"Not a thing."

Carter got up and went to the window. "How far is the town from here?"

"Fifteen miles."

"How big is it?"

"Hiva Faui? Three thousand that we know of. But

outside the town there may be three times that many Chinese.''

"How about the other islands . . . Natu Faui, Akau Faui, Tamau Faui?"

"A total estimated population for the entire island group, not including the personnel of this station, is around fourteen thousand people . . . whites, Chinese, and other Oriental extractions, and of course the Polys.''

Carter looked puzzled.

"Polynesians," Owen explained.

"I'd like to see it all."

"I don't understand," Fenster said.

"The town, the islands. I'd like to have the services of a helicopter and pilot, and I'd like to begin by looking over all the islands in the group.''

"Of course," Owen said. "Dick can take care of that for you.''

Fenster smiled and got to his feet. "First thing in the morning—"

"No," Carter said. "Now. This afternoon."

Fenster looked at Owen. "It'll be dark in a few hours.''

"Then we'd better hurry," Carter said.

For a moment no one said a thing, but then Owen finally nodded. "Have Bob Tieggs show him around.''

"I was planning on taking you into town myself, in the morning," Fenster said pointedly.

"I'd just as soon do this independently, Fenster. Nothing against you, of course, but I'd like to form my own views.''

Fenster scowled and was about to say something, but Owen did not give him a chance.

"Sounds like a good idea to me. Fresh perspective and all that. Tell Bob that Mr. Carter will meet him out on the pad in fifteen minutes.''

Fenster looked at them both, then stormed out of the office. When he was gone Owen shook his head.

"You don't particularly care for our chief of security."

"No," Carter said. He went over to the desk, picked up Owen's telephone, and unscrewed the mouthpiece cap.

"What the hell . . ." Owen said.

Carter soon had the instrument apart, and just behind the microphone was a tiny pickup and transmitting device.

"Good God," Owen whispered.

Carter pulled the unit out of the phone and put the instrument back together. He tossed the pickup across to the station manager. "Send that back to Washington. Have it looked at. Probably Chinese."

Owen looked from the transmitter to the telephone. "How long?"

Carter shrugged. "From the beginning, possibly. Or at least for the past two years."

"Whatever was discussed in this office got to . . ."

"Apparently. Whoever they are." Carter looked around the office. There were several file cabinets, two of them locked with heavy steel bars down the front of the drawers. "Who has access to your office?"

Owen started to say something but then changed his mind. "Everyone," he said after a moment.

"Change the locks on your safes, and at least once a day check your telephone. I'd also suggest you do the same in every office where sensitive material might be stored or discussed."

"It's a little late for that," Owen said glumly.

"They've got several slices of the pie, but that's no reason to give them the entire pantry."

While he had been talking, Carter had worked his way slowly over to the door. He jerked it open. No one was out there.

He turned back. "Bob Tieggs. How sure of him are you?"

Owen didn't seem to understand the question.

"Do you trust Duvall or Fenster? Completely?"

Owen smiled wanly. "Not really."

"How does Tieggs compare?"

"I get you. Bob Tieggs is a good, no-nonsense man."

"That's all I wanted to know. I'll see you later," Carter said. He left Owen's office, went down the hall, and stepped outside. A technician directed him across the compound back to the airfield where he was met a few minutes later in front of a hangar by a well-built young man with sand-colored hair and wide, deep blue eyes. There were laugh lines around his eyes.

"Bob Tieggs?" Carter asked.

"That's right," Tieggs said without warmth. "Fenster said you needed a pilot. I'll just get the chopper ready." He turned and went inside the hangar.

Carter followed him inside.

"Catch the doors, will you?" the pilot asked.

Carter found the switch for the doors and punched it. As they began to rumble open he went back to where Tieggs was readying a small Bell helicopter. The NASA symbol was painted on its fuselage. Their work here was under cover as a satellite tracking and receiving station for the space agency.

Tieggs had hooked a powered handcart to the front hitch on the helicopter, and he pulled the machine across the hangar and out into the hot afternoon sun.

"Where do you want to go?" the young man asked.

"I want to tour the islands."

Tieggs looked at his watch. "We'll have to hustle to finish by dark."

"I don't want to finish by dark."

Tieggs looked sharply at him. "There's nothing to see out there once the sun goes down. This place, the town, and perhaps a few native fires on some of the other islands is about all."

"We'll see," Carter said.

Within ten minutes Tieggs had warmed up the chopper, and they were rising away from the tracking station's air field and turning out toward the sea.

"Where to first?" Tieggs asked.

"Natu Faui," Carter said without hesitation.

Tieggs swung around toward the south, back over the island, and headed directly toward a group of islands several miles in the distance. Farther to the south, on the opposite end of their own island at the foot of a series of steep hills, the town of Hiva Faui gradually came into view. From here it looked like little more than a wide street that led up to a collection of white buildings scattered in and among the thick jungle growth. A thin plume of smoke rose from just beyond the town.

Carter pointed it out. "What's that?"

"Electrical generating plant. They burn everything from oil and coal to copra and wood."

They made it the remainder of the way across to Natu Faui in a few minutes, and Carter directed the pilot not to overfly the island, but to circle it at a distance of a quarter mile.

It was a very large island, even larger than Hiva Faui, but the western end of the island was dominated by a large volcano.

Once they had gotten around to that end of the island, they climbed so that they could see down into the smoking crater. It seemed to Carter as if it were still an active volcano.

"It is," Tieggs said. "But it hasn't blown its top for at least twenty-five years."

"Is it due?"

"The natives think so. Lots of superstition here."

"But natives live on this island?"

"At the eastern end," Tieggs said. "Not here. This end is very bad medicine."

They dropped down again and circled to the southwest side, and Carter had Tieggs set down on the wide beach. He got out of the chopper and motioned for the young man to shut it off.

"What's the idea?" Tieggs asked, climbing down.

"We're staying here until after dark, then we're going to fly over in a grid pattern."

"Listen, I don't know what you and Fenster have got cooked up, but as far as I'm concerned—"

"Fenster is an idiot who is no friend of mine. It's why I didn't take him along."

Tieggs looked at Carter for a moment. "No shit?"

Carter grinned. "You owe me an apology, Bob."

"I guess I do," Tieggs said, laughing.

THREE

The sun went down in the west, and it was almost instantly dark. Unlike northern latitudes where there were long twilights, in the tropics there generally was only daylight or darkness with very little in between. The night insects were very loud, competing with the sounds of the surf crashing against the barrier reef a few hundred yards offshore and another, lower pitched, more ominous rumble.

"Just what is it you have in mind to do up here, Mr. Carter?" Tieggs asked.

Carter had trudged up the gently sloping beach to the edge of the jungle. Tieggs had followed him.

"Quiet a minute," Carter whispered, straining to listen, to define the low-pitched rumbling.

Tieggs looked at him quizzically, then glanced back toward the helicopter.

"What is that?" Carter asked.

"Sir?" Tieggs asked, looking back.

"The rumbling. You can barely hear it."

Tieggs listened. "The volcano, I'd suspect," he said.

The volcano, Carter thought. Yes, but there was more there as well. Something steady, rhythmic, man-made. Something was running—some machinery

34

was operating somewhere at this end of the island—
and the ever present rumbling of the active volcano was
meant to mask the noise.

He looked back toward the southwest. The line
between where the sea ended and the darkening sky
began was nearly indistinct now. There was little to see
other than an amorphous blackness.

"Let's go," Carter said to the young pilot, who
looked at him for several long moments.

"Over the island? In a grid pattern?"

Carter nodded.

"What are we looking for, may I ask?"

"You may not, but if you see anything, let me
know," Carter said, smiling.

They went back to the helicopter, Tieggs grumbling,
and climbed in and strapped down.

Tieggs switched on the motor, and as the rotors
began to slowly gather speed, he flipped on the chopper's running lights. Carter reached out and shut them
off.

"No lights."

Tieggs opened his mouth but quickly had second
thoughts about what he wanted to say, and stopped
himself. He nodded, increased the power, cranked the
pitch control so that the blades bit deeper into the night
air, and they rose slowly into the star-studded sky.

Carter had to lean a little closer to Tieggs so that the
pilot could hear him. "Bring her around to the western
end of the island, and then give me a grid pattern, a few
hundred yards on a leg, over the island past the volcano."

Tieggs nodded, but still said nothing.

They followed the beach to the western end of the
island until it began curving north, then they climbed
so that they were skirting the western slopes of the
volcano. Carter watched intently as the dark jungle
flashed by beneath them.

At the northern side of the island, Tieggs expertly swung the chopper around in a tight arc, coming back over the island along a path a couple of hundred yards to the east of their first pass.

This time they were closer to the volcano, and the land rose up much more quickly. But Tieggs knew what he was doing. After a time, Carter forgot completely about the machine and the flying, and concentrated on what he was seeing below . . . or rather what he was not seeing.

There was nothing below them, absolutely nothing but the pitch-blackness of a tropical island at night.

Within a half hour their passes across the island had taken them up and over the center of the volcano's crater. Far below the lip of the mountain, Carter could just make out a dull red glow that backlit slowly rising steam, and then they were past and banking down the far slope.

Twenty minutes later, on one of their passes just east of the volcano, Tieggs sucked in his breath. Carter looked up.

"Uh-oh," the pilot said.

"What?"

For several moments they flew on in silence, Tieggs glancing from his instruments to the darkness outside. Then he looked over at Carter and shook his head. "If I didn't know any better I'd say we had passed over a fairly heavy electrical disturbance. All my instruments went crazy."

"Get us back over it," Carter ordered, swiveling around in his seat and trying to get a view of the jungle they had just flown over. "And bring us down."

Tieggs complied, swinging the chopper around and down in a very tight, descending arc, and soon they were skimming just over the tops of the trees.

"About here," Tieggs said. His gaze kept alternating between the jungle below and the instruments on his panel. But there was nothing. When they came to the beach, Tieggs swung the helicopter around and made another pass, but this time was the same as last; all the chopper's instruments remained normal.

"Maybe I was dreaming or something," Tieggs said.

"I don't think so, Bob," Carter said.

"What now? I can't find the spot."

"Let's get back."

"Hiva Faui? The base?"

Carter nodded. "I want to get into town."

"I thought you wanted a tour of the islands. All the islands."

"I've seen enough here."

"Yes, sir," Tieggs said as they burst across the beach, and he climbed to cruising altitude for the run back to the main island. "I can set you down in town if you'd like."

"I want to go in by jeep. I might want to stay the night."

"I'm a good jeep driver."

Carter laughed. "All right, you win, Bob. I'll let you drive me into town tonight."

Neither Owen nor Fenster were around when Carter and Tieggs returned to the station. But they had no trouble signing for a jeep from the motor pool section. Within ten minutes of the time they had set down, they had cleaned up and were headed into town.

It was a lovely tropical evening. There was a light ocean breeze, the humidity had tapered off, and the temperature had moderated.

They had each packed a bag with shaving gear and clean shorts and socks, but all the way in Tieggs kept telling Carter that there was nothing for him to see in the town.

"Nothing?" Carter asked, his right eyebrow raising.

"There's the booze shop, a couple of taverns, the

Chinese settlement up in the hills, and of course the hotel and Madame Leone's.''

"Madame Leone's?" Carter asked, laughing. "Is it what I think it might be?"

"Right on," Tieggs said with a grin.

"Any good?"

Tieggs laughed. "All depends upon your point of view. Madame Leone has eight girls—four of them white, four of them Chinese. If you're Chinese you love the white girls. If you're like us, then you'd probably like the Orientals. All pretty—more or less—and all clean—more than less."

"And that's it?"

"Except for the governor's mansion, which is strictly verboten for any of us—except for Mr. Owen from the station."

"Doesn't like Americans, I hear."

"Not at all. If it was in his power, he'd blow up the station and set us all adrift in a leaky boat."

"The obvious question—"

"No, sir. He and his people are definitely not behind our troubles at the station. He's been investigated up one side and down the other, not only by our own people—the naval intelligence boys—but by his own people."

"How do you know all this, Bob?"

Tieggs shrugged. "Hell, it's common knowledge. Everyone knows it."

"I see," Carter said.

"Then there's his wife," Tieggs said quietly, and Carter was certain a new note had crept into the young pilot's tone.

"The governor is married?"

"Yes, sir. He's a big, fat, ugly slob. But his wife . . . Gabrielle . . . now she's a beauty." Tieggs fell silent, apparently contemplating the French governor's wife's beauty.

They came down out of the hills along the coastal road from the tracking station, and Carter's first ground-level view of Hiva Faui, the capital city, was of a wide, dusty road that led past the municipal docks. There, opposite a half-dozen corrugated metal buildings that Carter supposed were used as warehouses, a miserable collection of rusty, down-at-the-heels fishing boats were tied.

Why a man would settle for a place like this was beyond Carter. But whatever Governor Rondine's crime against French society had been to stick him out here, it must have been very serious.

Past the warehouses and public commercial docks were the pleasure boat docks, and beyond them was a lovely white sand beach that led up to a wide square complete with a statue of a World War II soldier and a small fountain.

A line of well-kept buildings, one of them three stories tall, faced the square across a wide, cobbled street. Behind the buildings were mean-looking shanties and huts that ran all the way up to just below the crest of a flat-topped hill. At the top was a lovely old South Seas plantation house, its wide facade facing the sea. It reminded Carter of the big houses in Jamaica. It was ablaze with lights, and even from here Carter was certain he could see people on the wide porch.

Tieggs had stopped the jeep just down from the square, and he too was staring up at the governor's mansion.

"Something is going on up there," Carter said.

"He has parties all the time."

"With whom?" Carter asked, looking at the pilot. "I thought he hated Americans, and the only others here are the Chinese."

"There are a few Frenchmen and other foreigners, as well as a few very rich Chinese. Owen and sometimes Fenster are invited over, and of course there are the other islands in the Carolines, easily accessible by air.'' Tieggs looked back up. "The governor throws a mean party, from what I'm told. They come whenever he sends an invitation just to look at his wife. She's the most beautiful woman in all the islands.''

"I think we should pay the governor and his lovely wife a visit,'' Carter said.

"Sir?''

"Let's get to the hotel. I have to send a message. You and I are going to a party tonight.''

They were given a front room on the top floor with two large double beds, a huge ceiling fan, and a wonderful view of the park, the beach, and the pleasure boat docks. A cool breeze came in off the ocean, and Carter stripped down to his shorts and went out onto the balcony.

Tieggs's nostrils flared slightly at the sight of Wilhelmina and Hugo strapped to Carter's body, but he said nothing.

Carter picked up the phone, but before he rang for room service he turned back to Tieggs. "Bob, get back out to the base to my room and grab my tuxedo and black shoes. Get yourself a dark suit or tux and get back here.''

"I don't understand.''

"We're going to the governor's party.''

"But . . . but we haven't been invited.''

Carter laughed as he dialed. "We're going to crash it. I wouldn't want to miss the governor's wife for anything in the world.''

"Gabrielle,'' Tieggs said softly.

"Yes, Gabrielle. Now get going.'' The hotel room service clerk answered.

"This is Carter in three-oh-one. Bring me a bottle of your best dark rum, a pitcher of papaya juice, and some ice,'' Carter ordered in French.

"Merci, monsieur," the clerk said, and when Carter hung up and looked around, Tieggs was gone.

He got up and opened the door to their room so that he could look out into the corridor. It was dimly lit and empty. There was absolutely no noise in the hotel. The building could have been deserted.

He softly closed the door, lit a cigarette, then unholstered his Luger. He took his silencer from his trouser pocket, screwed it onto the end of the barrel, then pulled out several bills and laid them on the bureau. He went back out onto the balcony and sat down, his feet up on the low table.

Room service in the person of a very young Chinese boy showed up ten minutes later with his rum, juice, and ice. Carter tipped the boy, then mixed himself a large drink.

Back out on the balcony, the room lights out, he sat back, Wilhelmina on the chair beside him, and slowly sipped his drink as he watched the occasional car or passerby below on the street and in the square.

The town was very quiet at this time of night. But Carter suspected that was not normally the case. He supposed that what action there might normally be here in town tonight was centered up at the governor's mansion.

Contrary to what Tieggs thought, Carter suspected that Governor Rondine was somehow involved in the tracking site's problems. His motives were so patently obvious that the previous investigators had given the man the benefit of the doubt. Carter was not so inclined.

It was nearing nine o'clock when Carter heard a slight noise at the door. He picked up the Luger and slipped off the safety, then held the gun high against his chest. His back was to the door, but whoever was coming in from the corridor would present a clear target in silhouette.

He waited a full three seconds, then spun off the chair to the left, bringing his Luger up into a firing position. But if the door was open, then whoever had come in had first switched off the corridor lights, because there was nothing on the other side of the room but a vague darkness.

A flash of light and the whine of a bullet ricocheting off the balcony railing just above Carter came a moment later. Carter fired three shots in quick succession, one where the light flash had been and one on either side of it, then flattened himself on the balcony and waited.

A soft scraping noise came to him from the left, near the bed, but he resisted the urge to fire.

A truck rumbled by on the street below, turned the corner, beeped its horn, and then was gone.

A signal? Carter rolled to the right, back toward where he had been sitting, a split instant before a powerful flashlight was switched on and two shots were fired at the spot he had just been in.

Carter fired once above and to the right of the flashlight beam, then high and to the left. The second shot hit home. The flashlight flipped violently across the room, clattering against the wall, then something heavy thudded to the floor.

For a long time Carter remained where he was. He did not think it had been a trick, but he was not going to bet his life on it for a while yet.

Someone was out in the corridor, whistling, and then at the door.

"Hey, Carter, what happened to the lights?" Tieggs called out, pushing in the open door.

"Look out, Bob!" Carter shouted, but the door was all the way open before Tieggs understood that he might be in some danger. Tieggs thought fast, however, and quickly ducked back into the hallway.

An inert form was crumpled on the floor at the end of

the bed. It had not stirred. A small pool of blood had formed on the floor. Whoever it was was dead.

Carter got to his feet, keeping the Luger out ahead of him, and crossed to the body, which he carefully turned over. It was a Chinese man.

"It's all right now, Bob," Carter called. He switched on the room lights as Tieggs, carrying their clothes, came in, wide-eyed and panting.

"What the hell happened?"

"Someone doesn't like us, apparently," Carter said.

Tieggs came the rest of the way in and looked down at the body.

"Holy shit," he said.

"You know him?"

"You bet I do, Mr. Carter," Tieggs said, looking up. "It's Yun Lo."

"Duvall's batman? The one who tried to kill him?"

"One and the same."

FOUR

Carter found an empty room on the second floor and took one of its blankets. Back up in their own room he and Tieggs wrapped Yun Lo's body in the blanket, carried him back downstairs, and put him in the bed.

The man's body would not be found until tomorrow, and then there would be nothing official to connect his death with Carter.

Once again in their own room, they cleaned up the blood, and Carter collected his shell casings and reloaded his Luger. It had been a busy evening so far. He suspected it was going to get much busier before it was over.

He and Tieggs both took a shower and shaved, then dressed in their evening clothes.

"What's likely to happen is we'll be kicked out, if we're even allowed into the house in the first place," Tieggs said, combing his hair.

"I don't think so, Bob," Carter said. "Just stick with me at first until we're introduced."

"And then?"

Carter had finished with his bow tie. He turned around. "You don't have to come with me, you know. Just drop me off up there."

"I'll come," Tieggs said, suddenly grinning. "I

wouldn't miss it for the world. I just don't know why you want to go up there. I mean, what does it have to do with your investigation?''

"Are you ready?'' Carter asked, ignoring the question.

"Yeah . . . sure,'' Tieggs said.

Together they went downstairs, got into the jeep, and headed up the hill. A couple of Oriental men stood across the street at the edge of the square watching them. Other than that pair, the street was deserted.

At the end of the business district the road turned left up the steep hill, switching back and forth, following the terraced slope on which the shanties were built.

Near the top the hill began to flatten out, and the road curved around and headed directly toward the governor's mansion, which was contained in a large compound encircled by a tall, wire mesh fence.

The shanties had thinned out up there, but Carter suspected that farther back into the interior were more of them. Tieggs confirmed it.

"You can see them back in the hills on a fly-over if you watch for them.''

"Concealed in the trees?''

"The brush back there is pretty thick. Besides, they don't like company.''

"Who do you suppose Yun Lo worked for?'' Carter asked, changing the subject.

Tieggs glanced at him. They were approaching the compound's gate. Carter could see a couple of armed guards there.

"I think no one.''

"Then why did he try to kill me?''

"He knew you were an investigator here to look over the situation. He may have thought you'd come after him. Because of Handley.''

"The entire island knows I'm here?''

Tieggs smiled. "Every last one of them.''

They pulled up at the gate, armed guards approaching from both sides.

"*Bon soir*," Carter said and continued in French. "With my compliments to Governor Rondine and his wife, tell him Monsieur Nicholas Carter is here, with his driver."

For several long moments neither guard said or did a thing. They remained rooted to where they stood, staring at Carter as if he were some kind of apparition.

"Neither your governor nor I are patient men," Carter snapped.

The guard on the opposite side spun around and hurried into the guardhouse, and through the window Carter could see him pick up a telephone. Meanwhile, the other guard had placed his hand on the butt of his pistol at his hip.

In the overhead light from a stanchion above the gate, Carter could clearly see the man's face. He was a European, there was little doubt of that in Carter's mind, and yet there was an ever-so-slight Oriental cast to his features. Perhaps a grandparent had been Oriental.

The other one came from the guardhouse. He looked surprised.

"There is parking on the far side of the house, Monsieur Carter," he said.

"*Merci*," Carter replied.

"Please have your driver remain with your car, or if you wish, he may be dismissed, and a ride into town or out to the receiving station will be provided for you, sir."

"Of course," Carter said, inclining his head.

The gate swung open, and they drove through. They went up the road and around to the far side of the house where there was a large parking lot. It was filled with cars on one side, and fully a dozen small and medium-size helicopters occupied the other side and a wide, flat field beyond.

Tieggs whistled. "We knew choppers were brought in for these parties, but I never realized just how many."

"Lots of important people here tonight," Carter said. He looked over his shoulder. A separate road ran from the parking lot directly in front of the mansion and then connected with the road back to the gate.

"I know what you're going to say," Tieggs said heavily.

Carter looked back. "If you can't come in, I don't want you sitting around out here. It's too dangerous considering what almost happened tonight back at the hotel. No, Bob, I want you to go back."

"The hotel or the base?"

"The hotel. But watch your step. I won't be too late, I don't think. We can go back in the morning."

"All right," Tieggs said. He swung the jeep around and drove slowly down the front road, pulling up below the veranda. A few of the governor's guests glanced down in idle curiosity but then looked away.

"See you in a few hours," Carter said, and he adjusted the cuffs of his shirt as he mounted the steps.

An Oriental houseboy dressed in an immaculate white uniform met Carter at the head of the stairs.

"If you will just follow me, sir," he said, and he turned and moved into the house.

Carter followed him across the wide veranda, which was filled with men and women standing around drinking and talking. At one end of the veranda a pair of lovely young women were dispensing drinks to the guests, and at the other end of the balcony a seven-piece band was just beginning to set up.

Inside, the house was lit up and decorated for the party. In two of the rooms they passed through were service bars with young, lovely, female bartenders, and in another room an older black man was playing ragtime piano and singing.

From what Carter had seen so far, he guessed there were at least a hundred men and women there, about two thirds of them Oriental, the other third European.

They had come to the far side of the house, to another wide veranda, but this one faced the jungle. This balcony was only dimly lit and was quiet in comparison to the front area. There were about a dozen people seated around a wide, ornately carved coffee table. Two young girls, bare-breasted and wearing only sarongs, served drinks to the group.

Everyone stopped what they were doing when the houseboy led Carter around to the far side of the table. There sat one of the largest men Carter had ever seen.

Governor Albert Remi Rondine looked up, then smiled as he rose to his impressive six-feet-eight. Carter guessed the man to weigh in the neighborhood of 450 to 500 pounds. His hair, neatly trimmed, was jet black and slicked back with oil. He wore a small goatee, also well trimmed, and a pencil-thin mustache separated his bulbous lips from his grossly huge and misshapen nose.

The governor was, as Tieggs had promised, big, fat, and ugly.

"Mr. Nicholas Carter, I believe," the governor said in heavily accented English, his voice as rich and as deep as his appearance suggested it would be.

They shook hands.

"I heard you were having this little get-together, so I thought I might drop in," Carter said, glancing around at the others. No one was smiling.

"Please feel free to mingle, Mr. Carter. I am sure that some of my guests might find you amusing."

Carter grinned. "Actually, it was you I came to see,

Governor . . ." he said, but then his voice caught in his throat. To the governor's left, looking somewhat disconsolate, was an incredibly beautiful woman. She was neither European nor Oriental, but her olive skin bespoke an exotic background. Carter could not place the exquisite features. She had high, delicate cheekbones, lovely, large sloe eyes, full, moist lips, and a long, delicate neck. Her hair and eyes were very dark. She was dressed in a silk kimono, so he was not able to see her figure. But he guessed it was as lovely as her face.

"I had intended on calling you in within the next day or so," the governor said irritably. "I understand you only just arrived this afternoon."

"That's correct."

"Then there will be time enough for us to speak."

Carter focused on the gross man. The governor wore a white tropical suit with a white gauze shirt and a dark blue ascot. His dress was impeccable. Yet he gave Carter the impression of being a greasy, unkempt animal.

"On the contrary, Governor, there is no time. Americans are being killed."

"It is of little consequence to me," the governor shot back.

No one moved. Even his wife, who was about to raise her wineglass to her lips, stopped.

"It is of great consequence to me, sir," Carter said, choosing his words very carefully. "For when I find those responsible, I shall kill them." He nodded. Then he turned to the governor's wife. "It is a great pleasure for me to be here, Madame Rondine. I had heard how lovely you are, but even the most superlative claims do you no justice."

The woman stood up as the governor's complexion turned red.

Carter had struck a nerve. He started to step aside, half expecting the governor to take a swing at him, when his wife threw her wine into Carter's face.

"You arrogant American bastard," she said in English.

Carter held perfectly still for several long seconds, resisting the urge to turn around, or at the very least wipe his face. Instead he managed a thin smile.

"There was absolutely no offense meant, *madame*," he said in perfect French. "You are beautiful, and it is a fact. *Bon soir*."

He turned, inclined his head stiffly to the others around the table, and then nodded to the governor. "I will call on you at your office tomorrow," he said.

"I'll call you when I desire your presence—"

"I will see you tomorrow, Governor Rondine," Carter said, interrupting.

He turned on his heel and stalked off the veranda, going back through the house out to the front terrace. The houseboy who had shown him to the governor was at his elbow.

"Mr. Carter wishes perhaps for transportation to the base?"

"The hotel," Carter snapped.

"Very good, sir. It will be just a moment." The houseboy disappeared down the steps and into the darkness.

The band was playing a soft tune, and many of the couples were dancing. Carter went across to the bar and ordered a snifter of cognac. The young woman tending bar glanced up at someone across the veranda before she poured the drink. Evidently for permission.

The governor had quite a setup here, Carter thought angrily.

He sipped from his drink—it was an excellent cognac—then turned around so that he could see who

the woman had looked to for permission to serve him.
A tall man, dressed in a plain tuxedo, a small bulge at
his left armpit. One of the governor's goons. But if
nothing ever happened here that the governor was
involved with—nothing violent, that is—then why the
armed guards, why the security around the fence, and
why such a close watch on the Americans?

Carter raised his snifter in salute to the guard, who
stared back with no expression on his face, then took a
deep drink and put the glass back on the bar as the
houseboy came back up the stairs and looked around
for him.

The car was a big Mercedes limousine. It was parked
at the foot of the stairs. The houseboy opened the rear
door for Carter. When he was inside, even before the
door was fully closed, the limo sped down the road as if
it had been shot from a cannon, throwing Carter back
into his seat.

A partition of very dark glass separated the front seat
area from the rear, and Carter could not make out the
face of the driver. But they were going much too fast
for a simple lift into the hotel in town.

He thought about the switchback road that led
through the shantytown on the steep hill, and he began
to sweat.

As they approached the main gate and then flashed
past the bewildered guards, he fumbled for the door
latch, but just at that moment the electric door locks
snapped, blocking his escape.

For a moment Carter thought about shooting his way
out of the car, or pulling the panel from the door and
shorting the electric lock system, or trying to fire
through the back of the front seat in an attempt to kill or
wound the driver before they came to the more dangerous sections of the road down the hill.

He sat back instead, poured himself a drink from the

rear seat bar, then lit a cigarette.

If the governor meant to kill him, it would not be done so crudely as to destroy a very expensive car and a driver.

Presently they came to the first of the switchbacks on the narrow road, and the car slowed down. Carter allowed the faintest flicker of a smile to cross his lips. He crossed his legs and waited for the next move.

Governor Rondine had probably had this all planned out from the beginning. Merely to test Carter's mettle. Of the other investigators, Carter wondered how many had lost it at this stage.

Of course none of this proved a damned thing other than the well-known fact that the governor disliked Americans and especially disliked their presence here on his island kingdom. It did not in any way prove that the governor was involved with the troubles they had been having at the base—at least not directly.

Halfway down the hill the partition between the front and back silently lowered, and the car turned off the main road and edged back into a very narrow alleyway. Within fifty yards they were out of sight of the road as well as from anyone above or below.

The car stopped, and the driver turned into view. It was the governor's wife, Gabrielle Rondine. She was obviously frightened. Her lower lip was quivering, and her eyes were very wide.

"This *is* a surprise," Carter said.

"This is very important, Monsieur Carter. You must listen very carefully to me."

Carter stubbed out his cigarette and sat forward. "What is it?" he asked. "Are you in trouble?"

"No, but you are, *monsieur*. It is your base. It is under attack at this moment."

"Under attack . . . by natives?"

"Yes."

"How do you know this?"

"Never mind how I know it, I just do."

"Get me down to the hotel . . ."

"Your driver is not there. He was called away. He is on his way out to the base at this moment."

"Damn . . ."

"I will take you to your base, but in exchange you must help me, Monsieur Carter."

"What do you want?"

"I want to get away from here . . . from this place . . . from . . ."

"Your husband?"

"Yes," she said with much passion. "You must help me. You are the only one to stand up to him like that, and you did not panic when I drove fast down the hill—like the others."

"You drove them all?"

"No. But I knew about it. We all did."

There would be trouble with the State Department . . . in fact there would be hell to pay, Carter thought. But if he gave his word here now, David Hawk would back him up. He knew that for a certainty; it was why he made damned sure of what he was doing before he made a promise.

"Are you involved with the trouble against us?" Carter asked.

She shook her head.

"I must know the truth, Madame Rondine. If you are involved, there is nothing I can do for you."

"I am not involved!" she cried.

"I'll help you," Carter said. "Unlock the doors. I'm driving."

She did, and Carter jumped out.

"I know the roads better than you," she said. "I can get us there faster."

Carter didn't argue. He climbed into the passenger

seat, and she slammed the car in reverse, rocketing them out onto the main road, where she turned and then headed down the hill, sliding around the switchbacks and once or twice nearly losing it.

They careened through town, hitting nearly seventy going past the hotel, and then they were on the road out to the base, climbing along the cliffs that edged the sea, the powerful headlights slashing the darkness. Gabrielle was an expert driver, but the best they could do with the big car around some of the curves was forty or forty-five.

"How do you know the base is under attack?" Carter asked.

She did not dare glance away from the road, but she shrugged. "There was a telephone call just before you showed up. Albert took it."

"From who?"

"I don't know," she said. "But when he hung up he was very happy. He clapped his hands, and said you . . . Americans were getting it again."

"How did you know that my driver went back to the base?"

"I telephoned the hotel to tell him about the attack, but they said he left in a hurry after getting a telephone call."

Odd, Carter thought. He would have expected that Tieggs would have either come up to the governor's house to get him, or at the very least would have telephoned.

"Is the governor involved, then, with the attacks on the base?"

She glanced at Carter. "I do not know for sure, but I do not think so, *monsieur*. Albert is—how shall I say?—a coward. I do not think he would have the fortitude to do anything so covert. Besides, the commissioners were here, along with the SDECE. They found nothing. I think he is a bastard, but he is not attacking your people.''

''Then how did he know about tonight's attack?''

She laughed, the sound lovely. ''Albert knows everything that goes on here. Everything!''

Carter thought about that for a moment. ''About us, now?''

Gabrielle nodded solemnly. ''Yes, even this.''

Their headlights flashed across a fallen palm tree partially blocking the road and the wreckage of a jeep half in a ditch.

Gabrielle slammed on the brakes, and the big car fishtailed left and right, finally slewing around to a halt just before the tree.

Carter was out of the car in a second, his Luger in hand. Keeping low, he raced across the road and leaped down into the ditch.

Bob Tieggs lay half in and half out of the jeep, the windshield starred where he had crashed into it with his head.

This had been set up. The entire mess smelled of it.

Tieggs was unconscious, but he was breathing regularly, and his color did not seem bad. He had lost some blood from a number of superficial scalp wounds, but other than that—unless there was a serious concussion—Carter did not think he was hurt too seriously.

Gabrielle was at the edge of the road, and she looked down. ''Is it your driver?''

''Yes,'' Carter said, holstering his Luger. He gently picked Tieggs out of the wreckage of the jeep and brought him back up to the limousine. Gabrielle opened the rear door.

''Get our suitcases out of the jeep,'' he said.

She hurried back to the wrecked vehicle as Carter laid Tieggs in the back seat, then slammed the door.

Gabrielle was back a moment later with his and

Tieggs's overnight bags, which she tossed into the back on the other side, and then she climbed behind the wheel.

Carter jumped in the passenger side, Gabrielle maneuvered the big car around the fallen tree, and within a minute they were once again racing down the highway toward the base.

FIVE

When they were still a couple of miles away from the base, they could see a bright glow above the tree line. Carter powered down his window, and the sound of gunfire came to them on the night breeze.

Gabrielle sped up, the big car surging forward through the night. Carter took out his Luger, made sure there was a round in the chamber, and girded himself for the fight.

They could smell the smoke just before the last curve on the paved road, and then they were around the corner as four dark-skinned men, wearing nothing more than loincloths, came running down the hill through the open main gate.

Gabrielle let out a little squeak and slammed on the brakes. Carter leaned way out the window and fired three shots, picking off two of the natives. The third disappeared into the brush alongside the road, while the fourth turned back and hurried around the corner of the guardhouse.

The front wheels of the limo bumped up over the body of one of the natives, but Gabrielle had the car well under control as they came slowly onto the base.

"Wait here!" Carter snapped, and he leaped out

of the car, hurried around the front, and raced up the northwest perimeter road that led back behind the supply buildings, the A and B generator sheds, and eventually the cliffs along the northern tip of the island.

Most of the lights along the fence had been knocked out, so it was very dark along the back road with the thick jungle on one side of the tall wire mesh fence and the long, low buildings on the inside. A fire was burning somewhere toward the administration building, but the gunfire had ceased.

For just a moment Carter had the sickening feeling that everyone on the base had been killed, but then a siren kicked off, wailed for a few seconds, and shut down.

What sounded like Fenster's voice came booming over the public address system: "Mr. Owen, Mr. Owen, report to Administration. Mr Owen to Administration on the double. Baker team techs to Charlie dome. Baker team techs to Charlie dome."

An arrow smacked into the side of the building Carter was just passing, missing him by less than a foot. He peeled off to the left, turning sideways as he ran to present less of himself as a target as he searched the darkness ahead for a sign of the bowman. But there was nothing.

He pulled up short in a crouch, every sense tuned for a sign, any kind of a sign that the brown-skinned native was near.

There was something! Ahead and to the left. Carter leaped left as a second arrow ricocheted off the mesh of the fence. He fired one shot in the general direction from where he thought the arrow had been fired. He had no intention of killing the man. He just wanted to keep pressing him until they came to the far northern edge of the base. From the air, Carter had seen that the base was not fenced on this side. There was no need of a fence. The cliffs down to the ocean were at least two hundred feet high and a sheer drop.

Someone shouted something on the far side of the supply buildings, and two shots were fired.

Carter raced between the buildings, but at the front corner he stopped abruptly. Base personnel would be jumpy just now, and they would most likely shoot at almost anything that moved.

He eased around the corner. A pair of white-coveralled techs stood looking down toward the generator sheds. One of them was obviously wounded. Blood was dripping on the ground from his left elbow, which he held closely against his side.

"Which way did he go?" Carter shouted.

They both spun around, one of the techs bringing up his .45, the wounded man stumbling to the left.

"It's me . . . Nick Carter," Carter shouted, still half concealed behind the corner of the building.

"Jesus," the tech breathed in relief. He lowered his weapon.

Carter stepped away from the building.

"Jesus . . ." the tech said again, but then he stepped forward with a cough and fell on his face, an arrow sticking out of his back.

"Down! Get down!" Carter shouted to the other tech. He had not seen where the arrow had come from, but he fired a shot in the general vicinity of the generator sheds, the direction in which the techs had been looking.

The wounded tech looked from the direction of the generator sheds to Carter and back again as he stepped toward his fallen buddy.

"Get down, you stupid bastard!" Carter shouted again. He leaped away from the protection of the building and ran in a zigzag pattern toward the wounded man who seemed to be disoriented as he kept looking from his dead friend to the generator sheds.

The tech was less than ten feet from Carter when an arrow buried itself in his neck with a sickening sound, and the tech stumbled and fell to his knees, blood spurting everywhere as he tried to claw the arrow out of his throat.

Just beyond the second generator shed, at a distance of at least fifty yards, Carter spotted a movement, dark brown glinting dully in the red light from the burning barracks to the east.

Carter crouched in the classic shooter's stance, both arms straight out, and he squeezed off one shot from the Luger, then a second, and finally a third, the last hitting its mark. He was certain of it.

Both techs were dead; it took him only a second to make sure there was nothing he could do for either of them. Carter raced down the inner maintenance road past the last two supply buildings, and he slowed down as he passed the first generator shed.

There was a lot of shouting back up by the administration building. A car or truck horn was beeping, and he could hear the sound of some machinery running. It sounded oddly like a jackhammer.

The fire was beginning to die down, and some of the lights were coming back on up by the radomes, but where Carter was, it was very dark.

He had spotted the brown-skinned figure just beyond the second generator shed. But standing now between the two buildings, peering into the darkness, he could not be sure of anything he was seeing.

The native had been very accurate with his arrows. At this range, if he was still lurking around the corner of the generator building, he would not miss.

Carter stepped away from the building so that when he came around the corner he would not be right on top of the man if he were crouched right there.

Then Carter spotted the body lying in the grass just

off the road, in shadow, and he took a few steps closer.

Lying beside the native was a sturdy-looking bow and an animal-skin quiver that contained two arrows. As far as Carter could see, the man was not moving, but he saw no blood.

A car came around to the maintenance road, its headlights momentarily illuminating Carter's back. He turned around to see who was coming. At that moment he felt, rather than heard, a rapid movement to his left. He turned back in time to see the native rushing at him, a machete in his right hand.

Carter stepped back and to one side, but he was too late to avoid the native's callused foot to his right wrist, sending his Luger flying.

The native was momentarily off-balance. Carter managed a clumsy blow to the man's chest, spinning him backward.

The brown-skinned man recovered nicely and came at Carter with the machete raised high.

Carter easily sidestepped the charge and slipped Hugo out of the chamois sheath strapped to his right forearm.

The blade glinted brightly in the headlights of the car that had come to a halt somewhere behind him. The native, spotting the stiletto, pulled up short, much more wary now that he realized Carter was armed.

"I mean you no harm," Carter said in French. "But you must understand why I have to arrest you."

The native lunged, swinging the machete in a deadly underhanded sweep intended to disembowel. Carter leaped back and slashed downward, just catching the native's forearm with the tip of the blade.

Someone came running as the native began side-stepping to the left so that he would end up closer to the shadows at the side of the generator shed. That was when Carter knew he could take the man alive.

He lunged at the native, who swung back with the

machete but then spun around and started for the shadows. Carter was on him in an instant, grabbing his right arm and quickly bending it back so that the man lost his grip on the machete.

The native struggled around to face Carter, who let go, stepped back, and doubled up his fist, smashing it into the man's jaw. The native's head snapped back, and he crumpled to the ground.

"Monsieur Carter!" Gabrielle called out.

Carter turned around as Fenster, a grimly intent look on his face, blood running down from a shoulder wound, a .45 in his hand, came rushing at him, the automatic pointed at the downed native.

"Bastard!" Fenster shouted.

Carter put out his right foot, tripping Fenster, who went down hard. Then he kicked the gun out of the security chief's hand. The man howled in pain.

Gabrielle stood by the open door of the limousine. The big car's headlights illuminated the entire scene. She had evidently spotted him down here and had driven up from the main gate. He was surprised she had not been stopped. But then Fenster and his security people had evidently been too busy.

Carter found his Luger, then pulled the native to his feet. The brown-skinned man was just coming around, and as soon as his eyes focused he began to struggle. Carter thrust the Luger's barrel above the man's nose, directly between his eyes, and the native immediately settled down, his eyes rolling in hate and fear.

Fenster was just picking himself up. "You son-of-a-bitching bastard . . ." he started.

"Get hold of yourself, Fenster!" Carter barked. "We've got work to do!"

"The goddamned Poly . . ."

Carter looked at the security chief in disgust, then hauled the native around. With the Luger jammed into the little man's neck behind his right ear, he marched him back to the limo.

Without a word Gabrielle opened the rear door on the side opposite from where Tieggs lay, and Carter shoved the native inside and got in after him.

Fenster came over to the car. "Where the hell are you taking him?"

"The dispensary."

"He's not hurt."

"There are a few questions I'd like to ask him, Fenster," Carter snapped with exasperation. "This is the second all-out attack on this base. Hasn't it occurred to you to take a prisoner and question him? Or at the very least put up a helicopter to find out where the hell these people are coming from?"

Fenster climbed into the front seat as Gabrielle got in behind the wheel. He looked at her for a second or two, then inclined his head. "Mrs. Rondine. It is a surprise to see you out here this evening."

"Which way to the dispensary?" Carter asked from the back seat.

"It's up toward Administration," Fenster said, turning around. He spotted Tieggs on the back seat. "Christ! What happened to Bob?"

"He had an accident on the road coming up here."

"Turn around," Fenster instructed Gabrielle. "The dispensary is the other way up from the main gate."

There were several bodies lying here and there on and along the access roads up from the main gate toward the administration building area. Most of them were brown-skinned natives, however. Only a few technicians had been killed or wounded.

One of the barracks down the hill from the radomes had been set on fire. A half-dozen technicians were fighting the blaze, which had already consumed most of the building. A pump was going—the jackhammer noise—and they were playing streams of water on the adjacent buildings. The barracks was a lost cause.

Justin Owen was just coming out of the administration building when they pulled up across the street from it. The front of his khaki shirt was covered with blood.

Carter opened the door, got out, and pulled the native out after him.

"You got one of the bastards," the station manager shouted hoarsely as he hobbled across the street.

Gabrielle and Fenster had both gotten out of the car.

"Get up to the dispensary and get someone to come out for Tieggs," Carter told Fenster.

For just a moment it seemed as if the man would not take any orders from Carter, but then he turned on his heel and stalked up the walk and into the building.

Owen started to reach for his .45 when he got across the street, but Carter stopped him. "He's more valuable to us alive than dead."

They were speaking in English, and it did not appear that the native understood a word they were saying. But he was obviously very frightened. He kept looking up at the radomes and the antenna farm as if they were some sort of monsters that would leap out after him at any moment. He had shown a lot of courage facing Carter back at the generator sheds. But now he was frightened.

Curious, Carter thought. He looked around, suddenly conscious of the fact there were no Orientals around. Normally they were all over the place. But none were in sight at this moment. Even more curious.

"Good evening, Madame Rondine," Owen was saying, seeming to suddenly realize who she was. "I don't know if it is wise that you remain here. There still could be danger."

"She's staying with us," Carter said.

"What?" Owen asked. He was very confused by

everything that had happened, although he did not
appear to be wounded. The blood on his khakis looked
as if it had been splashed on him.

"She's leaving her husband. She's asked for politi-
cal asylum."

"Oh, Christ," Owen groaned. "We don't need this,
Carter."

"Later," Carter snapped. "For now I want this one
in the dispensary."

"Is he hurt?"

"No. I want to question him."

"The dispensary is full. We can use my office,"
Owen said distastefully.

Fenster came out of the dispensary with two men
who carried a stretcher.

They gently eased Tieggs out of the back seat and
carried him into the dispensary.

"What about him?" Fenster asked, looking at the
native.

"We're taking him to my office," Owen replied.

They went back across the road and into the administration building. Carter had to half drag, half
carry the native, who did not want to move no matter
how harshly he was prodded with the gun.

Inside, there were a number of people hurrying back
and forth. Owen stopped one of the techs.

"How about our communications dish?" he asked.

"We just about have it realigned, Mr. Owen," the
harried tech said.

"We'll have communications with the States within
the next half hour?"

"Or sooner."

"I want nothing out in the clear, do you understand
that? Not a damned thing."

"Yes, sir."

"Nothing by radio or by telephone. There are too
many ears out there."

"Yes, sir. As soon as the link is ready, we'll patch it through our crypto circuits."

"Good man," Owen said. "I want the *en clair* switchboard completely off line."

"Yes, sir," the technician said, and he hurried out of the building.

"This is the second time we've been caught with our pants down around our ankles. I don't want to broadcast it for any Tom, Dick, or Harry who has a communications receiver to hear."

"If you hadn't ordered it, I would have," Carter said.

Gabrielle had been standing silently a few feet from the men. Carter glanced at her, then back at Owen.

"Have you someplace for her to stay?" he asked.

"She can have the VIP quarters next to yours. But I don't think this is such a good idea."

"I'll take the responsibility that State will clear it," Carter said. He turned back to her. "Perhaps it would be best if you went up to your room."

Gabrielle managed a slight smile. "You want to question this man," she said. "How do you plan on accomplishing it?"

"I don't understand," Carter said.

"She means in what language," Fenster said. "Most of these Polys here don't speak English or French."

"He is correct," Gabrielle said. She looked at the native. "He probably speaks a pidgin Chinese, Japanese, and Malaysian."

"Fenster?" Carter asked. The security chief shook his head. "Owen?" The station manager shook his head.

"I speak it," Gabrielle said softly.

"Right," Carter said. It was about what he had suspected. There was something drastically wrong here. A security chief who didn't know what the hell he was doing. A station manager who was inept. Orientals who were everywhere except when trouble came. Natives who came and went at will. A French governor who was obviously involved with the troubles the base was having, yet nothing could be proved. And now the governor's wife showing up as the only translator.

They all went into Owen's office. The native seemed much calmer now that they were out of sight of the radomes and antenna farm.

Carter had him sit in a chair facing the window. The blinds were drawn.

"Ask him why his people attacked this base," Carter told Gabrielle.

She came up beside the man and looked into his eyes. He stared up at her, unblinking, unsmiling. She spoke, the pidgin language a soft, tonal series of vowel sounds punctuated by glottal stops.

The native just looked at her, but he made no move to answer or even indicate that he had understood.

"Tell him I will open these blinds, and something very bad will fall upon him," Carter said.

Gabrielle seemed confused.

"Just tell him that," Carter insisted.

She did, and the change in his expression was noticeable. Still, however, he said nothing.

Carter went around Owen's desk and, keeping his eye on the native, slowly raised the blinds all the way. The change in the native's expression this time was startling. His apparent self-confidence and lack of understanding instantly melted away, changing into abject fear.

"He will be sent to that place," Carter shouted, pointing out the window to the radomes and antenna farm.

Gabrielle told the native what Carter had said. The man shook his head and babbled something.

"He begs you on his family's heads and on the great

god Hiva Maui Hiva—which I think is the volcano on Natu Faui—not to do this to him.''

''Why did his people attack this station?'' Carter asked.

Gabrielle repeated the question, but the native kept shaking his head and repeating his plea.

Carter lowered the blinds, and the man calmed down. Gabrielle repeated the question.

For several moments it seemed as if the native was not going to answer them, but then he launched into a long, very involved explanation of some sort. Several times Gabrielle stopped him and asked him something else. Each time it produced another string of babble.

At length he fell quiet, and Gabrielle looked up. She seemed uncertain. It raised the hair on the nape of Carter's neck.

''His people attacked this base twice because each time the god of Hiva Maui Hiva appeared and told them to do so.''

Carter waited for her to go on. But she did not. ''That's it?'' he asked. ''All that?''

''He kept repeating it, and I asked if he meant the volcano was active . . . if the god spoke to his people through flame and lava. But he said no. The god himself appeared.''

''What else?'' Carter asked. Fenster had a sneer on his lips, and Owen was clearly confused.

''I asked him if the god had come as a sign. A bird flying at night. A shark. Some other sign. But he insisted the god came to them in person. In a ghostly light at night,'' Gabrielle said. This last seemed to disturb her the most.

''Holy shit,'' Fenster swore.

They all turned as the native flipped off the chair onto the floor, blood gushing from between his clenched teeth as he choked.

''Christ!'' Carter shouted, throwing himself down

beside the native. "Get a medic over here on the double!"

The native had bitten completely through his tongue. A large piece of it hung by a few tatters against his cheek. His eyes were open wide and shining.

Carter tried to roll him over on his stomach so that the vast amount of blood pumping from his severed tongue would not choke him to death. But the man resisted. When Carter finally did get him over, the native kept taking deep, rasping breaths, forcing the blood down his windpipe and into his lungs. Drowning himself in his own blood.

Fenster had rushed out the door, but long before he returned with the medic, the native shuddered, then lay still.

SIX

After the native's body had been removed from Owen's office, they all stood around staring at the huge pool of blood until Owen finally went to the door and shouted for his batman, Huang Chou.

One of the technicians hurrying down the corridor looked back. "They're all gone, sir," he said.

Owen stepped out into the hallway. "What did you say?"

"They're all gone, Mr. Owen. There isn't one Chinese on the base."

Owen walked in glum silence back into his office.

Carter had poured them each a stiff shot of bourbon. "They knew about the attack before it came."

"It would seem so," Fenster said, taking his drink.

"Why didn't you know?"

"We never expected anything like that to happen the first time and certainly not a second time. We weren't even looking."

"It's all right," Carter said tiredly. He glanced at his watch. It was after one in the morning. It seemed like years since he had last slept. "As soon as your people get back, we'll know how they got in and out undetected."

"What?" Fenster asked.

"Your patrols," Carter said. "The people you sent after the natives."

Fenster said nothing.

"You did send up a chopper or at least a couple of men on foot to follow them?"

Fenster shook his head. "There was too much confusion," he said. "In the darkness we didn't know who was hurt, who was killed, or what was going on."

"Damn," Carter swore. "Is there another chopper pilot? I can fly, but I want to concentrate on the ground."

"I can fly the helicopter," Fenster said. "But it's no use. We wouldn't see a damned thing out there. It's too dark."

"You run a curious security operation here, Fenster."

"I don't have to take that, Carter. Not from you or anyone else. If you want my resignation, you have it. Otherwise, I'll take you over to Natu Faui in the morning. Only that won't do you much good. We've tried it before."

The man was probably right, Carter thought. The damage had already been done. There was very little to be done about it tonight. In the morning he would go over to the island. One way or another he was going to get to the bottom of this. And very quickly.

He turned to Owen. "Where is your crypto section?"

"Crypto?" Owen asked.

"Your comm center. I have to talk with Washington this morning."

"If you want my resignation, you can have it here and now. You don't have to complain to Washington."

"Shut up, Fenster," Carter snapped. "If and when I want your resignation, you'll be the first to know, I assure you."

"This isn't going to help us," Owen said wearily. "We have at least four men dead, another dozen wounded."

"Six," Carter said. He told Owen about the two techs by the generator sheds.

"We're going to have to get help from Washington, or we're going to have to shut down. The men won't stand for it. They'll quit, contract or no. This isn't the military. We're all civilians."

"I'll see what can be done," Carter said.

"Duvall quit. He was just outside. He had shot and killed two natives. He just turned around and told me to shove this place. He was quitting."

"The comm center," Carter prompted.

"Across the way in Engineering Able. Next to the antenna farm," Owen said. "But I'll have to go with you. They won't let you in otherwise."

"Fine," Carter said. He turned back to Fenster. "Would you show Madame Rondine to her quarters in the VIP building?"

Fenster nodded.

"Afterward, I want you and your people to question every single person on this base. I want as accurate a picture of what happened, when it happened, who was killed, and who was wounded, as possible."

Again Fenster nodded. "What time do you want to fly over to Natu Faui?"

"Oh-eight-hundred," Carter said. "That'll give you a chance to do what you have to do, and it'll give us all a chance to get a few hours' sleep."

"I'll have some clothing sent up to your quarters, Madame Rondine," Owen said.

"I would appreciate it, Mr. Owen," she said. She nodded to Carter, then left with Fenster.

"We're in for some trouble from the governor and his people before this is all over," Owen said.

"Most likely," Carter said. "I'll see what I can do

with State on that score as well.''

They went across to the engineering building, to a back, windowless room where they signed in to the top-secret electronic cryptographic room. Here classified messages were sent back and forth between this station and the Central Intelligence Agency, the Pentagon, and to a special circuit addressed to the State Department but in actuality relayed through AXE on Dupont Circle.

A young technician was there on duty. He was extremely nervous and kept fumbling with an M-2 carbine, a thirty-round clip in place.

''You're going to shoot someone if you keep doing what you're doing, son,'' Carter said.

The young man nearly jumped out of his skin.

Owen led him back to the door. ''I want you to wait outside, Brad. I don't want anyone coming in here and bothering us for the next . . .'' He turned back to Carter.

''Half hour, forty-five minutes.''

''All right?'' Owen asked, turning back to the young man.

''Yes, sir,'' the tech said crisply, and he stepped outside, the thick metal security door clicking shut behind him.

''You want me in or out, Carter?'' Owen asked.

''You can stay,'' Carter said. ''Just don't read over my shoulder. Anyone else read these circuits?''

''Not outside this room . . . other than the addressees.''

''Good,'' Carter said. He sat himself down in front of the machine marked for the State Department, opened the circuit, and typed in his recognition code and the For-Your-Eyes-Only designation for David Hawk.

The reply came within a second or two, and the indicator for him to stand by came a moment later.

Carter sat back and lit a cigarette.

"Coffee?" Owen asked.

"Sure."

The station manager poured them both a cup, handed Carter his, then went back to the desk, sat down, and put his feet up. It was approaching noon in Washington, so Hawk would certainly be at his desk.

"I get the impression you've done this before," Owen said from over the rim of his cup.

"Done what?" Carter asked.

"I don't know what you people call it . . . missions, assignments, jobs. Whatever."

"I don't know what you're talking about."

"I think you do."

Carter looked at him. "You're going to have to hold yourself together a little bit longer."

"What the hell is that supposed to mean?" Owen snapped, sitting forward.

"It means if you fold on me now, like Duvall folded on you, my job will become difficult if not impossible. If that happens, I have a fair idea a lot of people will be killed."

"Agency hoopla . . ."

"I don't engage in histrionics, Justin," Carter snapped. He was very tired and at the thin edge of becoming nasty.

"I see . . ."

The teletype in front of Carter rang five bells, the indication of a highest-priority incoming. He swiveled around to it after noting the impressed look on Owen's face.

FOR YOUR EYES ONLY NICK CARTER N-3

FRENCH HAVE LODGED AN UN-SPECIFIED PROTEST OUR AMBAS-

SADOR   PARIS   QUERY—ANY
KNOWLEDGE YOUR STATION

HAWK

Quickly Carter teletyped that he had full knowledge
of the protest, which involved kidnapping.

The machine was silent for a few seconds, and
Carter could almost see David Hawk, his thick shock
of white hair mussed, the ever present cigar clenched in
his teeth, staring at the teletype as he thought out
Carter's message.

QUERY—PROGRESS REPORT YOUR
ASSIGNMENT—DO YOU REQUIRE
ASSISTANCE

NOT REALLY KIDNAPPING—BUT
CHARGE WILL BE SAME

As quickly and as succinctly as he could, Carter
teletyped a full report on what had happened since he
had gotten there, including the transport pilot's obser-
vation that the Orientals ran the place, his initial meeting and first impressions of Duvall, Fenster, and
Owen, his subsequent flyover of Natu Hiva with
Tieggs, and then his meeting with the governor, the
trip back with Gabrielle Rondine, and the attack on the
base.

REQUEST   STATE   DEPARTMENT
CLEARANCE ASYLUM FOR GAB-
RIELLE RONDINE   QUERY   RE-
QUEST POSITION OF NEAREST U.S.
NUKE SUB

This time the circuit was quiet for at least ten minutes, and Owen was beginning to get nervous by the time the five-bell signal rang again.

Carter turned back to the machine as it spat out the latitude and longitude of the U.S.S. *Starfish*, then translated that into a mileage figure from Hiva Faui.

The *Starfish*, with its full complement of men and nuclear weapons, was about 1700 nautical miles away. Estimated time of arrival, according to Hawk, was in thirty hours, which meant the sub could make, submerged, better than fifty-five knots. Amazing.

REQUEST STARFISH ON SITE FOR
POSSIBLE ASSISTANCE UP TO BUT
NOT INCLUDING NUCLEAR STRIKE

The teletype was still for another two or three minutes. But then the final message clattered:

STARFISH YOURS

Carter cut the circuit, then cranked the paper out of the teletype machine and ran it through the shredder.

Owen had poured himself another cup of terrible coffee, and he had lit a cigar. He sat behind the desk watching Carter's every move.

"Well?" he said. "Do the peons get let in on it? Or do we have to guess?"

"Help is on its way, Justin," Carter said.

Owen looked up hopefully.

"Thirty, maybe thirty-five hours at the most, and this will all be over."

"Are the Marines landing? Is that it?"

"Something like that."

"But I don't get told."

"You don't get told," Carter said. He didn't want to start a panic. If there was a leak on the base, Carter wanted to make absolutely sure that the imminent arrival of the *Starfish* did not get out. Owen was the head man . . . it would begin with him.

"I see," Owen said, getting up from behind the desk. He held the cigar tightly between his teeth at the side of his mouth, then unlocked the steel door and stepped outside. Carter followed him, the young technician slipping back into the room.

Halfway down the corridor Carter stopped the station manager.

"It's not what you think, Justin," he said.

"What's not what I think?"

Carter looked into his eyes. "You signed on as a satellite tracking and receiving station manager. Am I correct?"

Owen nodded.

"I'm going to give that back to you."

Owen started to protest, but Carter held him off.

"Stay out of my business, Justin, and I'll give you your business back to you on a silver platter. Is it a deal?"

Owen hesitated.

Carter stuck out his hand. "Is it a deal?" he asked. "You let me do my job, and I'll give you your job in return?"

After a very long, pregnant silence, Owen managed a slight smile. He shook hands with Carter. "It's a deal, Carter," he said. "But then I don't have much of a choice, do I?"

Carter shook his head.

Owen laughed, then turned and walked down the corridor and out the door into the warm night air.

The engineering building had quieted down, and after a few moments Carter followed the station manager out of the building.

There was still a lot of activity on the base, but it was not as frantic as before. The fire in the barracks building was all but out, and there were only two men watching it now, with one fire unit.

As he crossed the main street, Carter looked down toward the main gate. A pair of trucks had been pulled up tailgate to tailgate in front of the main gate, and there were several armed men down there watching for another attack—an event that was highly unlikely to occur tonight.

Beyond the dining hall, Carter crossed the far street and entered the administration building, taking the back stairs up to the VIP housing area.

In his own room he peeled off his clothing and his weapons, then stepped into a scalding hot shower, which he ended with an icy cold blast.

After he dried off, brushed his teeth, and downed a quick shot of brandy from the bottle on his dresser, he crawled into bed and was asleep almost before his head hit the pillow.

It was just dawn when Gabrielle Rondine climbed into bed with Carter, her breasts pressed against his back, her long legs entwined with his, and her lips brushing his ear.

He had been in a deep sleep but was awake in an instant, and he turned around to face her. She was smiling.

"Good morning," she said, her voice husky.

If her face was beautiful, her body was gorgeous. Her skin was a soft, olive color, her shoulders tiny, her arms long and delicately formed. Her breasts were small, the nipples already erect, and just below the slight roundness of her belly, her jet black pubic hair had been partially shaved . . . evidently so that she could wear a very brief bikini. Her legs were very long and lovely.

"I'm surprised you're here, like this," Carter said. He reached out and caressed the nipple of her left breast with his fingertips. She shivered.

"I am not," she said. "The moment I set eyes on you on the back veranda, I knew that I would be . . . with you."

For a long time they just looked at each other. Gabrielle's eyes were very large and shining, her lips full.

"Was it very bad with him?"

"Yes," she said softly.

"Why . . . how is it you came to be with him?"

For a second or two Carter didn't think she was going to answer him, and he started to ask her a second time, when she began.

"I am a criminal," she said. "It was either go to jail or come with him to this place."

"What did you do?"

"I killed a man. A very bad man who raped me."

"When was this?"

"Years ago," she said. Tears were forming in her eyes, and she pulled away and started to get out of the bed, but Carter pulled her back.

"Tell me about it, Gabrielle," Carter said gently. "Get it out of your system."

She was shaking as she lay back, her hands on her stomach. Carter propped himself up on one elbow beside her.

"I was little—eight years old—when my father was killed in Africa. I am Algerian. After that happened, my mother moved us from Algiers to Paris. The next year she met Henri, a Frenchman, and they were married."

Gabrielle turned her head so that she could look directly into Carter's eyes. "I was nine then. When I came home from school one afternoon my mother was out shopping, and Henri was there.

"He waited until I had gone upstairs to my room to change my clothes. He came in wearing only his robe, and I was in my panties."

Tears were filling her eyes now.

"I asked him what he was doing in my room, but he just smiled at me and said it would be all right. He just wanted to talk to me . . . father to daughter.

"I told him to leave, but he made me sit on the bed with him, and he started telling me about how sometimes my mother didn't kiss him enough—that was how he worded it, I remember—and that made him sad and angry. And when he was sad and angry he might be forced to hurt her very badly.

"But he said it didn't have to be that way if only I would help him."

Carter knew what was coming, of course. It was not a new story. She had been used by that man and then later by Rondine.

"That first day he only made me . . . touch him. I was so ashamed, but I was so afraid that he would hurt my mother, or do something very bad to me, that I did not tell. Each time he came to my room I told myself it would never happen again, and that soon I would tell what he made me do. I was just a skinny little girl and he was a big man—with a temper."

"You don't have to go on . . ." Carter started to say, but she kept talking as if she had not heard him.

"Later he would make me take off all my clothes, and he would fondle me as I was playing with him. It made him happier, he told me. Made him less likely to hurt my mother.

"Then, about a year after it had started, my mother almost caught us, and it stopped for a long time. Until I was thirteen or fourteen, and had begun to look like a woman.

"It started the same way, only this time it progressed much faster."

Gabrielle shut her eyes.

"I came home from school one afternoon—my mother worked during the day at a café, and Henri worked in a factory at night. He was there in my bed, naked.

"I told him I would call the police, but he said they would never believe me. And even if he did go to jail because of me, when he got out he would kill me *and* my mother.

"I was standing near my bed while we were talking, and when he saw me glance toward the doorway, he leaped up and grabbed me. Henri was a very strong man . . ."

Gabrielle's chest was heaving as she relived that time.

"When it was over he went into his own bedroom and went to sleep. I went down into the kitchen, got the biggest knife I could find, and came back upstairs and killed him. I kept stabbing him over and over, and there was a lot of blood.

"My mother came home an hour later, and I told her everything. We left that very night for Algiers, where we hid in a very bad section of the city."

"Rondine was there?" Carter asked.

Gabrielle opened her eyes and nodded. "He was the consul there. My mother worked as a housekeeper in his big mansion. There came the day when the police in Algiers were notified by the police in Paris to be on the lookout for me. My mother didn't know what to do, so she went to Albert and told him everything.

"I was brought to see him, and he immediately agreed to help. My mother and I were sent out here to these islands. Albert joined us a year later, and within two months my mother became ill and died. Albert said I was to be his wife, and if I tired of that he would send me back to France to stand trial for murder."

She shuddered. "I could not stand it any longer," she said. "And now I do not want to go back to France."

"You won't," Carter said. "Nor do you have to go

to bed with me to get my help.''

She managed a smile, and she reached out and caressed his cheek. ''I am not here because of that,'' she said. ''I am here because you will be the first man I have been with whom I *wanted* to be with.''

This was all wrong, Carter thought. She was a very vulnerable woman, and for a moment he felt as if he were taking advantage of her, no matter what she said. But the feeling lasted only a moment as she sat up and pushed him back gently.

''Relax,'' she cooed. She kissed his eyelids, then his nose, and finally his lips, her right leg moving against his.

At first he just lay there, but soon she was kissing his neck, and behind his ears, her breath warm and close and lightly scented with cinnamon, and he began to respond. He drew her close, crushing her breasts against his chest, and they kissed deeply, his tongue exploring hers, his hands on her back, then down the incredibly long, soft small of her back to her lovely derrière.

''Oh . . . God,'' she breathed. ''Oh . . . God . . .''

Carter eased her over on her back, and kissed her breasts, taking the nipples in his mouth and using his tongue to stimulate her.

Her chest was heaving now, her legs spread, as she moved against him.

He kissed the spot between her breasts and then worked downward to her navel, and even lower, his hands on the mounds of her buttocks.

She wanted to scream as she moved back and forth; he could feel it as a vibration in her entire body, her legs around his shoulders, her hands grasping his head.

But then she was pulling him away, up, on top of her. She reached down and grabbed him, guiding him inside her, her long, lovely legs wrapped tightly around his waist.

Carter forced himself to slow down. He looked down at her. She was staring up at him, a half smile on her full, sensuous lips.

He began to move then, carefully, deeply, and with each movement she rose up to meet him, a half moan escaping from her lips with each thrust.

"This is . . . the way it is . . . always supposed to be, *mon chéri*," she breathed.

Carter kissed her eyes, and her lips.

"I have always dreamed of this . . ."

He sensed that she had been on the verge from the very beginning. Her breathing was even more shallow, much faster, and her eyes shone.

"Gabrielle," he whispered her name. "Sweet Gabrielle."

"Oh . . . yes," she cried as Carter thrust deeper, and harder and faster, her body continuing to rise against his, her legs tightening around his waist, her fingernails clawing at his back.

And then they were both coming, a moan escaping Carter's lips, as she clung to him with everything in her power.

Afterward they lay in each other's arms. Carter smoked a cigarette while Gabrielle looked up at him.

"It was very good for me, Nick. Was it for you?"

He smiled at her, happy he had given her pleasure. "It was very good for me, Gabrielle. Very good."

SEVEN

Fenster had set out armed perimeter guards, especially along the northeastern side of the base where they thought they had found a path up from the sea that the natives might have taken.

He had also sent out a heavily armed patrol down the highway toward town to remove the tree blocking the road and to retrieve Tieggs's jeep.

The news was not very good that morning. Fenster and Owen were seated together in the dining hall when Carter and Gabrielle, dressed in khakis that Owen had sent up, came in. The large room fell silent as they crossed, everyone's eyes glued to Gabrielle.

"Good morning, Madame Rondine," Owen said. "Carter."

They sat down, and the place finally got back to normal. Gabrielle was amused, and she managed a slight smile.

But neither Owen nor Fenster was smiling. "We found Duvall," Owen said.

"In town?" Carter asked.

The station manager shook his head. He seemed very grim. "He was just beyond where we found Bob's jeep."

Carter started to ask what Duvall was doing there, but then he understood.

"His throat was cut, and he was hanging by his ankles from the branch of a tree," Owen said.

"I've never seen so much blood," Fenster added.

Gabrielle sat forward. "Pardon me, Mr. Owen, but who discovered this man's body?"

Owen's eyes narrowed, but he shrugged and looked to Fenster. "I don't know."

"One of my security people found him," Fenster said. "But I was out there this morning myself."

"Underneath the . . . body . . . where the blood collected. Was there . . ." She was having a little trouble, and the looks on Owen's and Fenster's faces were not helping much.

"What is it?" Carter asked gently.

"Beneath the body, were there large palm leaves to collect the blood?"

It was Fenster's turn to sit up. "There were, come to think of it. Struck me as very strange."

"It was a ritual murder then," Gabrielle said. "Mr. Duvall was sacrificed."

Owen and Fenster looked at each other. "I knew it was natives who had done this," Fenster said. "But I thought it was their radicals."

"No," Gabrielle said with certainty. "Your Mr. Duvall was killed in a religious ceremony."

"How do you know all this?" Carter asked.

She looked at him and smiled. "Through the years here, with little or nothing to occupy my time, I have become something of an expert on the local Polynesians . . . their cultures, their languages, their heritage."

"I would have thought they'd hold their religious ceremonies in their villages."

"Normally they would. But this particular sacrifice is designed to take place in the field . . . the field of battle against a particularly hated and feared enemy. It gives them strength while at the same time draining the blood of their foes.''

''We're the hated enemy?'' Owen asked.

''Apparently so,'' Gabrielle said, turning to him.

''But why? What in God's name have we ever done to these people?''

It all suddenly fell into place for Carter . . . or very nearly all of it. The *Starfish* would be here in about twenty-four hours. He had until then to find out if he was right, or if he was way off base.

''I cannot answer that, Mr. Owen.''

Fenster got up. ''I'll have the chopper ready for you anytime you want to go.''

''What is this?'' Gabrielle asked, looking from Fenster to Carter.

''I'll just have some coffee and be right with you,'' Carter said, and Fenster turned and left.

Owen got up. ''Be careful out there, Carter. If something goes wrong, there won't be a damn thing we can do for you.''

''I won't be long.''

''What I don't understand is what the hell you hope to accomplish by going over there.''

''Over where?'' Gabrielle asked.

Owen turned to her. ''He wants to go over to Natu Faui. After what happened here . . . I don't know. But I think he'll end up like poor Handley Duvall.''

She turned to Carter. ''Why *are* you going over there this morning, Nick?''

''I want to look around,'' Carter said.

''I'm coming with you.''

''Absolutely not—'' Carter started to protest, but she interrupted him.

''Not only can't you speak their language, you have no idea as to their culture, their villages, their ways of thinking . . . their gods to whom they make sacrifices.''

She was making perfect sense, of course, Carter realized. And they would have the helicopter to get the hell out of there in a big hurry if anything went wrong.

Carter smiled. "You win," he said.

Owen shook his head. "You're crazy. First you show up with the French governor's wife, and now you plan on carting her off to an island inhabited by hostile natives." He shook his head again. "Christ," he said, and he turned and left the dining hall.

"He is a very distraught man," Gabrielle said.

"I think he and Duvall were good friends."

"It is very sad."

For just a moment, looking at her profile, her complexion glowing, Carter felt a sense of wonder at the way things were turning out. A few hours after meeting, they had made love, and it had been near perfect.

Gabrielle turned back, breaking the spell, and a quizzical expression came into her eyes.

"Is something wrong?" she asked. She glanced toward the door and then back.

Carter shook his head and smiled. "I was just thinking about this morning," he said.

She reached out for his hand. "Was it good for you?"

Carter smiled and nodded. "And for you?" She nodded.

After they had some breakfast, Carter got a .45 automatic and holster for Gabrielle, who assured him she knew how to use the weapon, and then they went over to the flight line where Fenster was waiting with the helicopter.

The security chief came around the chopper when he saw who had come with Carter. His eyes strayed to the .45 strapped at her hip.

"I'm not taking her," he said.

"Why not?" Gabrielle asked.

"She's not coming, Carter," Fenster said, ignoring

her. "If something should happen over there, and she were to get hurt, there'd be hell to pay."

"I tried to convince her to stay behind, but she wouldn't listen to me," Carter said, opening the passenger side door of the helicopter. He helped Gabrielle up into the rear seat.

Fenster just stared at them. He was fuming.

Carter turned back. "Don't just stand there. I'd like to get over and back before lunch."

"What did Justin have to say about her?"

"He just shook his head and said we were crazy," Carter said. He climbed up into the front passenger seat and strapped in. "Are you going to take us over, or do we find another pilot?"

Fenster slapped the side of his leg in frustration, but he finished his walk-around inspection of the helicopter. Then he climbed into the pilot's side and fastened his seat belt. He flipped a series of switches, and then the starter motor, and the big rotor began spinning.

"What part of the island do you want to see?" Fenster shouted over the din of the blades.

"Put us down on the beach at the southwest end of the island."

Fenster looked sharply at him. "Near the volcano?"

Carter nodded. "That's right."

"If the natives are already pumped up, that'll be no place to wander around. The volcano is holy to them."

"Right," Carter said.

Gabrielle sat forward. "What is wrong?" she shouted.

Carter turned around to her. "Are you ready?" he said. She nodded, and Carter turned back to Fenster. "Let's go."

Fenster sighed deeply, but then they lifted off, straight above the base, and headed south. At the edge of the island Carter could see Fenster's security people along the low cliffs. He could also see that the cliffs had been undercut by the wave action. He pointed it out to Fenster.

"We think they hide their canoes in the caves and then climb up," the security chief shouted.

"No way of patrolling the area from the sea?"

"There are tens of thousands of little holes and caves. At night it would be impossible to see much of anything."

Fenster swung them directly south, and in the distance they could see the volcano on Natu Faui in the haze.

Two miles out, they spotted the first of the native outrigger canoes strung out toward Natu Faui.

"That's why it's impossible to detect an attack ahead of time," Fenster said, pointing down at them.

"What are they doing? Fishing?"

"Some of them. Others are pearl diving. Sponge diving."

Carter looked at them. "And some of them are killers."

"It would appear all of them are killers, if Mrs. Rondine was correct about the religious killing."

"Bring us a little lower," Carter said.

"They won't like it. Our rotor wash screws them up."

"I don't like killing."

Fenster wanted to say something in return—Carter could see it in his eyes—but he held his tongue and brought them down directly over a half dozen of the canoes.

Carter pulled out the binoculars, and as they passed, he looked down into each boat. He had expected to possibly catch one of the boatloads of natives unawares and find them with weapons. He was not prepared for what he did see, however. Every canoe was loaded with weapons: bows and arrows, machetes, spearguns. But there did not seem to be firearms of any kind.

Carter asked Fenster about it as they climbed back up.

"They are a very independent people, from what I know," he said. "The French leave them alone as long as they don't arm themselves with modern weapons. The bows and arrows and other weapons were used to hunt with . . . until now."

Ahead, for as far as they could see toward Natu Faui, was a virtual armada of canoes.

"The only thing to do will be either to wipe out the entire island or put a garrison on it," Fenster was saying.

The fact that the natives carried only primitive weapons did not fit in with Carter's idea of what was happening on these islands. Yet he still felt he was on the right track.

"It'll come to that, you'll see," Fenster said. "And it won't be our Navy who'll do it. It'll have to be the French. They know how to deal with problems like that."

Another thing bothering Carter was the fact that last night during the attack there were no Orientals to be found anywhere on the base. But this morning they had been back, not as if nothing had happened, but as if they had been there all along, fighting side by side with the rest of the base personnel.

They were approaching the southwestern beaches of Natu Faui, and Fenster was looking at Carter as if he were expecting something. He had evidently asked a question, but Carter had not heard him.

"I'm sorry," Carter said. "I was thinking. You asked me something?"

"I said that after all that has happened, I don't want to set you down on this island. It's simply too dangerous."

"We're going down."

"I would be remiss in my duty as security chief if I

let anything happen to you," Fenster said, and he started to peel off to the west, around in a big circle away from the island.

"You set this machine down anywhere but where I asked you to take me, and I will break both of your arms, Richard," Carter said, keeping his voice even.

Fenster flinched as if about to be struck, but he brought the chopper back on course. "This is insanity, you know that."

They were approaching the beach. The volcano loomed well above them, a few miles inland.

"If it was just you, it'd be one thing. But dragging the governor's wife along . . ."

Carter took out his Luger, ejected the clip, then worked the slide mechanism back and forth a couple of times. He replaced the clip, levered a round into the firing chamber, made sure the safety was engaged, and slid the weapon back into its holster at his belt beneath his shirt.

During all that, Fenster nervously brought them down for a jerky landing on the beach halfway between the water and the thick wall of jungle.

He shut down the engine, and in the silence, Carter opened his door and unbuckled.

"I want you to stay here with the chopper. We might have to beat a hasty retreat."

"What are you planning on doing?"

"We're going inland. There's something I have to see. If you hear any shooting, start the engine and get ready to lift off."

Fenster looked from Carter to the jungle and back. "Where inland? How far? And just what is it you're going after? I don't understand any of this."

"I'm not going to stop and explain. Just be here when we get back. Understand?"

Fenster wanted to argue, but again he held his tongue. He nodded.

Carter got out of the machine and helped Gabrielle down.

"We may have to hike several miles each way," he said to her. "Do you think you're up to it?"

She smiled. "I'll manage," she said.

"Keep your eyes open," Carter said to Fenster. "We're heading directly inland. If anything happens out here, come in toward us. Let us know what's going on."

Fenster swore under his breath, but he nodded. "How long do you suppose you'll be?"

"Several hours," Carter said. "Keep a sharp watch." He took Gabrielle's arm, and they went up the beach until they found a break in the thick vegetation that allowed them to penetrate the jungle.

There was so much undergrowth that the going was very difficult for the first few hundred yards. But then the ground became much harder as it began to rise toward the volcano, and the growth began to thin out.

They stopped after a half hour to catch their breath. Carter figured they had come about a third of the way to the general vicinity where the helicopter instruments had gone crazy when he had flown over with Tieggs.

Gabrielle's face was covered with a thin sheen of perspiration. It had been the same earlier this morning when they had made love in his room. She had been like a sensual animal then. Now she seemed like some sort of a sleek jungle cat. She was strange and very sad in some respects, but incredibly lovely and innocent all at the same moment.

"Just where is it we are going, Nick?" she asked.

"It's farther inland. Possibly an hour or more away from here."

"But what is it you are seeking? Why this place? What has drawn you here?"

Quickly he told her about his search of this end of the island with Bob Tieggs and of the odd readings on the helicopter's instruments.

"So you think there is something going on up here? Something electrical, evidently, if it had such an effect on your machine's instruments."

"Something very powerful."

"Do you have any ideas?"

"Radar, perhaps," Carter said. "We may have crossed its beam. I don't know. It's why I'm here now."

"You think it has something to do with the native attacks?"

"I don't know, Gabrielle."

"But it is why you have brought me along. If we find something, I will be able to translate."

"What could make them hate our installation so much? What could drive them to such attacks?"

"I do not know, Nick. But it certainly has something to do with their religion. In their minds, your people have evidently committed some sacrilege."

The helicopter, trailing thick black smoke, clattered overhead then disappeared to the north, the noise of its engine fading almost to nothing, but then it came back.

"What is happening?" Gabrielle cried.

Carter looked around for a climbable tree as the chopper clattered overhead again. This time it was going much more slowly, however, as if it were searching for something or someone, and almost immediately it swung back again toward the north.

There was a bright flash followed by an explosion. The machine rolled over on its side and dived.

Seconds later the dull thump of an explosion came to them through the trees, and they headed in a dead run toward the north.

EIGHT

The helicopter, or what was left of it, had come down in a thicket at the edge of a small clearing on the side of a lava flow. The fire was still far too intense for them to get very close to the wreckage. There was no doubt in Carter's mind that Fenster was dead. No one could have survived the explosion and fire.

Carter was certain that the machine had not exploded because of some malfunction. He could have sworn that just before the chopper exploded there had been a bright flash, as if a small ground-to-air missile had homed in on it.

But why had he gone up in the first place? Had the natives come back to the island? Or had someone or something else come in on him?

"What happened here, Nick?" Gabrielle asked.

"I don't know for sure," he said. "But it's a safe bet the natives didn't do this."

She looked sharply at him. "Who then?" she asked. "There is no one else here. The natives, your people, my people."

"And the Chinese," Carter reminded her. "Let's not forget them, shall we?" If it had been a missile, Fenster never had a chance. But the ship had been trailing smoke when they first saw it. Something had happened down on the beach. He immediately thought about pheasant hunting. The natives had possibly flushed him up into the air, and then the missile was fired. From inland.

It was only a few minutes after nine, but already the morning was becoming brutally hot. To the west the volcano towered over them. Straight inland, among hills rich with vegetation, was something that had interfered with the helicopter's flight instruments.

"How are we going to get back?" Gabrielle asked. She had been staring forlornly at the flaming wreckage.

"We'll worry about that later. I still have a job to do, and I intend doing it."

"But we cannot continue."

Carter took her hands. This had all been too much for her. He should have known better than to bring her along this morning. After her escape from her husband and the attack on the base, she was just overloaded.

He did not think the natives would harm her. They evidently were being directed against the American installation and the Americans, not the French. Besides, she would be known here. And she knew their language and customs.

"Go back to the beach and wait for me there. I'll be a few hours."

"No," she cried.

"You can talk to the natives. We'll need a canoe to take us back to Hiva Faui. Tell them I am French as well. By the time they realize where I am I'll be on my way back."

"No," she said again. "I am not leaving without you. You will come back to the beach with me. Together we will find a canoe and we will return to Hiva Faui."

"I have a job to do, Gabrielle. You can return to the

beach or come with me. The beach is the easier alternative.''

''You're determined?''

''Yes.''

''Then I will come with you,'' she said. She glanced up at the volcano. ''Soon we will be on holy ground. It will be very dangerous if we are caught here. You will need help.''

''How do you know this, Gabrielle?''

''That it is dangerous here? Everyone talks about it. Everyone knows that this end of the island is powerful. The last people who were here were killed when the volcano had a minor eruption. An act of nature or of an angry god. It makes little difference.''

Carter looked over at the still burning helicopter. ''And that?'' he asked. ''An act of an angry god?''

''Perhaps,'' she said defiantly. ''The natives will think so.''

''Right,'' Carter said. The submarine would be here in less than twenty-four hours. He wanted to be ready for it. ''Are you sure you don't want to return to the beach?''

She shook her head.

''Okay,'' he said. ''It's this way.'' He turned inland, skirting the burning chopper, and followed the general curve of the hills that led up toward the smoking crater of the volcano.

At times they scrambled over old lava flows filled with cracks and loose rocks. At other times, where enough topsoil had collected, they had to push their way through dense undergrowth.

It had become very hot and extremely humid. Their clothing clung to them, and mosquitoes and other flying insects followed them in swarms.

Gabrielle kept up with no problem, although she was sweating just as profusely as Carter.

''I've lived in this heat for a long time, you must

remember," she said once when they stopped to rest.

Carter had lit a cigarette, and she looked at him with some amusement.

"What is it?" he asked.

They had stopped at a small spring from which clear, very cold water bubbled. It was pleasant in the shade of several large trees.

"Smoking is one of many things these people do not understand about us. It is one habit they have not picked up."

Carter was about to reply that they were smart, but an odd, high-pitched keening sound came to him from a distance. He looked up, cocking his head so that he could better hear the faint sound.

Gabrielle heard it as well, and she got up from where she had been leaning against the bole of a tree.

"What is it?" Carter asked.

"It is them. The natives. It is their trail hunt cry."

"It's us they're after," Carter said.

"They have picked up our trail from where the helicopter crashed."

Carter ground out his cigarette, then pocketed the butt. "We're not too far from what I wanted to see. We'll continue."

"It will not take them long to catch up with us," Gabrielle said, following him away from the spring, the sun still off to their right as they headed inland.

"Where won't they follow us? The volcano?"

They had gone a hundred yards or so when she grabbed his arm and pulled him around.

"They would not follow us up the side of the volcano, it is true," Gabrielle said. "But for good reason. Anyone who goes up there is a dead person."

"Superstition," Carter said, glancing up toward the peak. Smoke curled lazily from the crater, which had to be three or four thousand feet above the floor of the jungle.

"Yes, there is a lot of superstition here that the Japanese could not control, nor could we. My government has sent three separate teams of geologists up there. Set them down near the summit by helicopter. The first team simply disappeared. Their wrecked helicopter was spotted on the western slope near the peak. The second team . . . all but the pilot were overcome by toxic fumes. The pilot managed to take off and radio back what happened, but then he too passed out and crashed into the sea."

"How long ago was that?" Carter asked.

"This all happened a couple of years ago," she said. "The last team, about a year ago, came with gas masks. The volcano erupted while they were camped near the top. It is believed they were all killed instantly in their sleep. No one knows for sure. Neither their bodies nor their helicopter were found."

The howling noises were much closer now, but Carter figured he and Gabrielle were coming up fast on the area he and Tieggs had pinpointed the previous night.

If the natives would not follow them up the side of the volcano, he decided that he and Gabrielle could at least start up the lower slopes where they could conceal themselves until after dark when they could make their way back to the beaches.

"You see, there is much more than superstition up there."

"Then we'll only go a short distance up and hide until after dark," Carter said, and he struck out once again to the north, roughly parallel to the curve of the volcano, Gabrielle right behind him, and the natives farther back . . . but not much farther.

Ten minutes later they came around a wide outcropping of rock and a dozen yards or so below them Carter spotted a trail through a narrow opening in the undergrowth.

The natives were very close behind them, and Carter figured they would come into sight at any moment.

"Down there," he said, grabbing Gabrielle's arm and propelling her down the hill and into the underbrush.

Twice she nearly stumbled and fell, but each time Carter held her up and she regained her footing on the rocky ground.

"What is it?" she cried.

"A path," Carter said as they pushed the rest of the way through the thick growth, finally coming out onto a wide, apparently often used trail through the jungle. From here it appeared as if the trail more or less paralleled their own path from the downed helicopter just below the first foothills leading up to the volcano.

The place he and Tieggs had chanced upon the other night would be just a short distance farther north, he figured.

"Are you all right, Gabrielle?" he asked. "Can you make it just a little farther?"

She nodded. "But we had better do it quickly, Nick. They will be on us any second."

"This way," he said, and he headed north in a long-legged stride that Gabrielle could barely keep up with.

Within a quarter of a mile the trail turned sharply downhill to the east but then immediately opened into a fairly wide natural amphitheater of grass that was ringed on three sides by huge, overhanging trees. From the air there would be little to see down here, Carter realized. It was perfect for a concealed meeting.

At the far end of the depression, which was set into the side of the hill, was a strange grouping of large boulders, one of which was unnaturally flat, much like an altar stone used for sacrifices in some ancient cultures.

Carter and Gabrielle hurried around the rim of the bowl to the flat boulder, but a few yards from it,

Gabrielle stopped short, her right hand going to her mouth as she stifled a cry.

The flat boulder was splattered and stained with blood. Carter stepped up to it. The stench this close was almost overpowering. Even the trampled, hard-packed earth at the base of the stone was stained with blood, and insects worked at bits of rotting tissue.

It was definitely a sacrificial altar. And Carter suspected, from the stone's general shape, that ordinary animals were not the victims. This place was for human sacrifice.

The natives were very close now. Probably on the path. They were howling and whistling and hooting as if on a hunting drive, beating the bush for animals that would be driven toward waiting marksmen.

Which is exactly what was going to happen, Carter suddenly realized as several dozen natives, who had been hiding along the rim of the depression, popped up, bows drawn.

"Down!" Carter shouted as he spun around and raced the few steps to Gabrielle.

He pushed her out of the way as a dozen arrows thudded into the ground where she had been standing.

Other arrows barely missed them as they ducked behind the altar stone.

Gabrielle was terrified, and she was shaking and retching as they crouched in the horrible odors of death and decay.

The arrows had stopped flying, at least for the moment, but a high-pitched crying began that echoed eerily throughout the amphitheater.

Carter peered out around the edge of the stone. Other natives had joined the first, and he estimated that now there were at least a hundred of them, all armed with bows and arrows. They ringed the depression on three sides.

But not on the fourth, Carter noticed as he ducked

back and looked up into the rocks behind the altar.

He almost missed the chance reflection of sunlight off something very shiny. But then his eyes came back to it. High in the rocks was a piece of metal or glass. Something fairly large but partially camouflaged. Something definitely man-made, but not by these natives.

He searched the jumble of rocks to the left and right as well, and he spotted two more round, intensely shiny objects. They were like flat pieces of glass or plastic embedded in the stone.

Definitely not natural. And definitely not a product of the skills of these islanders.

The crying became louder and then changed into some sort of a rhythmic chant.

Carter peered out around the stone in time to see the natives slowly coming down the hill, down toward the altar as they chanted.

"It is their death march for criminals," Gabrielle said at his side.

"No appeals?" Carter asked, again studying the rocks at the back of the amphitheater.

"We are here, so we are guilty as far as they are concerned. This is hallowed ground."

Carter picked out at least two possible paths up through the rocks to the rim seventy or eighty feet above them. Beyond the rim were the hills that led even farther up onto the slopes of the volcano. They would be exposed only for the first few yards, and then they would be behind the larger boulders.

"I want you to say something to them," Carter said.

"What?" Gabrielle asked, confused. "We're going to surrender? They might not kill us at first. I could talk to them. They might listen."

"Tell them that if they do not surrender to us, we will call upon our gods to strike them down."

"I do not understand, Nick."

"Just do it," Carter said. "Loudly so that they can hear you."

She was very confused. But she peered over the top of the stone at the advancing natives still chanting the death march. She glanced back at Carter, who nodded for her to go ahead.

Gabrielle turned back and shouted something, and the chanting stopped. She shouted something else as Carter pulled Pierre, the tiny gas bomb, from his crotch.

She finished speaking, and the chanting resumed even louder than before.

"It did not do any good, Nick. They are still coming."

"Warn them once more," Carter said.

Doubtfully she shouted out the warning again; this time the chanting did not stop.

Carter armed the tiny gas bomb, and without getting up he lobbed it well over the altar toward the advancing natives.

The gas bomb made no noise, and the gas was colorless and odorless. It worked on the central nervous system and was very fast and extremely effective.

A silence suddenly fell over the amphitheater. Gabrielle let out a little gasp, and Carter peered around the edge of the altar stone. A half-dozen natives lay on the ground. They were dead from the effects of the gas. The others had fallen back and were looking with awe from their fallen comrades to the altar stone.

Carter ducked back, pulling Gabrielle with him. He pointed up toward the rocks. "Do you think you can make it up there?"

"What did you do, Nick?"

"There's no time for explanations now," Carter snapped. "Can you climb?"

She looked doubtfully up at the rocks, but she nodded. "I think so," she said.

"Good. Then go, *now*. I'll be right after you."

"I . . . I . . ." she stammered.

"Now, Gabrielle, before it's too late," Carter said.

She kissed him on the cheek, then scrambled from the altar, jumped up on the rocks, and began climbing. Carter had taken out his Luger. He turned back and peered around the side of the altar as a cry went up.

Several natives brought up their bows.

Carter fired three shots, each hitting one of the islanders. The others fell back. Carter turned and scrambled up to where Gabrielle had gone, then he fired two more shots over the natives and leaped up on the rocks.

Several arrows clattered on the boulders below him a second or two later, but he was within the protection of the large rocks now.

Gabrielle was about ten or fifteen feet above him, pulling herself up hand-over-hand with little or no problem.

She reached the top and pulled herself over. Carter pulled himself over right behind her.

Below, the natives were streaming out of the amphitheater and heading around on the path. They would be up this far very quickly.

Carter got up and helped Gabrielle to her feet. "Up," he said, and they both turned and crashed their way into the jungle that led up the steep hills.

Far above them the uppermost slopes of the volcano were visible against the backdrop of an incredibly blue sky. Smoke poured from the crater. It looked as if the volcano were coming alive and would soon erupt.

They did not have much of a choice at this point, however, Carter figured. It was either here with the islanders or up there with the volcano.

About a hundred yards above the rocky rim of the amphitheater, Gabrielle tripped over something and went sprawling on her hands and knees.

Far below them and off to the east they could hear the natives screaming and wailing.

Carter helped the woman to her feet and was about to continue up the hill when he spotted what she had tripped over. He bent down to have a closer look.

It was a cable. An electrical cable with thick rubber insulation. It had been buried beneath the jungle soil, but a section of it had worked its way to the surface.

Carter tugged on the loop, and the cable snaked out of the ground toward the rocky rim of the amphitheater and up the hill before it snagged on something and he could pull no more out of the ground.

"Wire," Gabrielle said. "What is it here for? Did your people put it here?"

"Not us," Carter said, looking up the hill in the direction the wire led.

It was evidently connected to something in the amphitheater. The three shiny objects high on the face of the rocks came to mind immediately. Whatever those devices were connected to was somewhere up this hill in the direction the cable ran.

"Then who? Surely not the natives."

"I don't know," Carter said. "But we're going to find out."

They continued up the hill, sweat pouring off them in the intense midmorning heat, the sounds of the natives far below them becoming fainter and fainter.

"Oh!" Gabrielle cried twenty minutes later as she crested the first hill.

Carter was up with her a moment later. He had to smile. He had found what he had come looking for. Or at least he had found a sign of it.

In the hollow of a half-rotted tree, which had apparently been struck by lightning some time ago, was a small dish antenna that was painted with a camouflage pattern.

"I do not understand any of this, Nick," Gabrielle

said, looking from the dish to Carter and back again. "Does this have something to do with your base?"

"I don't think so," Carter said, approaching the dish. He turned so that he was facing in exactly the same direction as the dish was pointed.

They were high enough in the hills now so that they could see a long distance across the valley. Far off, out across the jungle, Carter thought he could see something, but he wasn't sure.

He turned back to the dish antenna and hunched down beside it. There were markings on the lip of the dish and along one of the struts. They were on small identification plates. One contained a long serial number. The other contained a number of figures. Chinese characters. The dish was Chinese.

NINE

It was night. They had remained by the communications dish through the remainder of the morning and into the afternoon. Whoever had installed the device had undoubtedly convinced the natives that here was holy ground . . . that this was the work of gods.

Carter figured that as long as the natives believed that, he and Gabrielle would be perfectly safe where they were. The natives would be too frightened to come this far.

And he had been right. No one came up after them, although they heard the islanders howling and wailing far down the hill for most of the afternoon.

Around three, Carter and Gabrielle had managed to slip down the hill to the spring, where they drank their fill. They gathered a few coconuts and some kiwi fruit, then made their way back up the hill to the communications dish.

Several times Gabrielle questioned Carter's insistence that they remain by the dish, and each time he gave her the same answer.

"We'll wait until after dark. Then we'll go back down the hill if nothing happens."

"What do you expect is going to happen?" she asked.

"I don't know," Carter admitted. He looked out across the long valley for another glimpse of whatever it was he thought he had seen earlier, but it was gone—or never had been there in the first place.

The sun had gone down an hour earlier, and some clouds had moved in from the west, gradually filling the sky and blotting out their meager starlight.

The temperature had not dropped with the sun, and the humidity had risen sharply. As they sat looking down the hill, their backs to the tree, they were bathed in their own sweat.

Gabrielle was becoming impatient. "It is dark now, Nick," she said. "You said we would go when it became dark."

Carter nodded, somewhat disappointed. He had hoped something would have gone on tonight down in the amphitheater. Yet he was not really surprised it had not. The attack on the base had come yesterday. He suspected it had originated here. Another ceremony probably would not occur so soon. Eventually another would occur, but. . . .

Carter sat forward at the same time Gabrielle did.

"Nick?" she cried.

"I see it, I see it," he said. Below, directly down the hill toward the amphitheater, a long string of pinpoint lights bobbed and moved, much like a troop of glowing army ants. They were torches, Carter figured. The natives were gathering in the amphitheater. There *would* be another ceremony tonight!

"They're coming together for another sacrifice," Gabrielle said with a shudder.

There would probably be another attack on the base tonight, Carter thought. This time, however, if Fenster's people were on the ball, little or no damage would be done.

The islanders were gearing up for something. For some reason they had stepped up their pressure on the base. But that made little or no sense to Carter.

If the Chinese did have a monitoring station here on this island—a station to monitor what the American spy satellite was receiving—why would they want to harass the site? It could only result in the U.S. Navy coming ashore in force here sooner or later and discovering what was going on. There was no way the Chinese could prevent that, short of instigating an international incident.

For a half hour a steady procession of torches marched from inland, presumably up the wide path Carter and Gabrielle had discovered, and gathered within the bowl of the amphitheater.

A bright yellow glow from the hundreds of torches rose from the depression.

"We can get out of here now," Gabrielle said at Carter's shoulder.

He looked at her.

"They are all there. They are busy. They would never notice us."

"I came here to find out what's going on, and I'll remain until I do. The Chinese Communists are on this island. I think they're behind the attacks on our base. I want to know why, and I want to stop them."

"Chinese, Americans, what difference does it make?" Gabrielle asked. "It is all for war . . ."

Carter was no longer paying any attention to her. His eyes had strayed to the communications dish. A pencil-thin ruby red light was hitting the central horn of the dish. He got up and went over to it, then knelt down beside the dish and sighted from beside the horn toward the inland area where he thought he had seen something earlier.

The pencil-thin line of laser light disappeared into the distance. It was a laser communications link.

He looked back down to the amphitheater as all the torches went out, plunging the valley into darkness. In the next moment, however, an eerie white light rose from the depression.

Carter stood up.

"I do not like this, Nick . . ." Gabrielle said. She too got to her feet.

Even as he watched, Carter could see the white light shifting back and forth below. It reminded him of the shifting projector light of a drive-in movie when the scenes changed. Movies.

He turned back to the communications dish receiving the laser beam signal and slowly put his hand out so that he interrupted the signal. At the same time he looked down toward the amphitheater. As his hand blocked the laser signal, the white light rising from the valley was abruptly cut off. When he pulled his hand back, the light returned.

The Chinese were sending signals from some inland installation to this dish. From here they were sent by cable down to the amphitheater, probably to the three shiny devices he had noticed in the rock.

They were sending signals. What sort of signals?

"We're getting out of here right now," Carter said.

"Now you are talking sense," Gabrielle said.

Together they started down the hill. The going was very slow because of the darkness and the loose rocks. But they had the shifting white lights from the amphitheater to guide them until about the halfway point, when Gabrielle suddenly stopped.

"This is close enough," she said.

Carter looked from the valley back up to her.

"We'll have to go along the hill until we find the path on the other side of the meeting place."

Carter came back up to her. She had been so strong when she had escaped from her husband and when she had volunteered to come here with him. But now it seemed as if she were falling apart.

He took her by the shoulders and looked into her

eyes in the dim light. "You've got to hold yourself together a little while longer, Gabrielle," he said.

"We have to get out of here, Nick. Before they work themselves into another frenzy. They will kill anything in their path."

"We have to find out what is driving them to it."

"Their sacrifices!"

"That's part of it. But there's more."

"No!"

"Then you can remain here by yourself. Or go down to the beach," Carter said. He turned and headed down the hill.

"Nick!" she cried.

He ignored her as he carefully picked his way through the darkness. A minute or two later she was beside him without a word. He reached out and took her hand in his, and together they hurried the rest of the way down the hill to within a hundred yards of the rock outcropping at the back rim of the amphitheater.

If there were any sentries, Carter figured they would be stationed around the rim of the depression. So he and Gabrielle would have to be very careful from this point forward.

Carter took out his stiletto, the blade gleaming dully in the shadowy light coming from below, and motioned for Gabrielle to make absolutely no noise even though the natives had begun to howl and scream below.

She came very close to him, her lips just at his right ear, and she whispered, "They will not be able to hear us."

"There may be guards," Carter whispered back. "Stay here for a moment. Don't move, and don't make any noise. I'm going to see if anyone is there."

"Let's get out of here," she whispered, but Carter crouched down and silently worked his way the rest of the distance down the hill.

There was no one there as far as he could determine. Not on the rim above the rocks. Not within the thick undergrowth to both approaches.

The crowd below was screaming in what sounded like rage, the noise almost deafening.

Keeping low, Carter worked his way to the edge of the rim, and flattening his body against a large boulder, he peered down into the amphitheater.

He had been prepared for almost anything except what he was seeing. The three shiny objects high in the rocks were projection lenses that presented a three-dimensional holographic image just above the altar stone.

That part did not surprise Carter. It was what he expected the dish antenna was being used for. But the images being projected were stunning.

It was the same scene, or a variation of the same scene, repeated over and over, in which terrible things were being done by American technicians to native women and children within the radomes of the American satellite receiving station.

The women, and in some cases young girls, were being raped by big, burly technicians. Some of the children were being cut open, their organs being tacked up on poles. In one scene the livers of two young native girls were force-fed to their mothers and sisters.

At each outrage a fresh cry of anger and despair arose from the native gathering.

At least a part of the Chinese strategy suddenly became clear to Carter. The natives would continue to riot against the American receiving site. If any of them were captured and questioned, even under drugs, they would all tell the same quasi-religious story about how their gods told them what the satellite receiving base was for.

Even if the American forces totally wiped out this island or relocated its population, the Chinese could move to another island and begin the same strategy all over again.

Gabrielle eased down beside him and peered over the edge, her breath catching in her throat as she realized what was and had been happening here.

Carter eased back away from the edge, his stomach churning. It had not been the islanders' fault. They were nothing more than simple natives who had been used as pawns in an international game of intrigue . . . a game that was being played with absolutely no scruples or concern for a naïve, trusting people.

Away from the rim, Carter and Gabrielle scrambled back up the hill to the spot where the cable had come to the surface. Carter pulled about fifteen feet of it clear from the dirt, then with his stiletto he cut one end and then the other, pulling out a fifteen-foot-long piece.

The shifting white light below in the amphitheater went out when he cut the first wire, and a silence almost as loud as the cries of outrage descended on the jungle.

Carter reburied the two severed ends and smoothed out the disturbed earth so that it would be difficult or impossible to tell where the cable had been cut.

Then he sheathed his stiletto, coiled up the fifteen-foot section of wire, and headed east, the direction from where the laser signal had been transmitted.

A rising murmur was coming from the amphitheater. Gabrielle looked over her shoulder into the darkness. It would not be long before the islanders decided to do something. They would probably head across to Hiva Faui tonight for another attack on the base.

It would be very bad for them to be caught anywhere near the beach right now, Carter knew, so they headed partway up the hill, then struck out toward the northeast, giving the amphitheater a wide berth. A couple of miles farther, they turned just south of east, walking toward where Carter figured the Chinese transmitting antenna was located.

He had no real idea what they would find, although he suspected there would be some sort of a small outpost and probably on holy ground so that the natives would not get too close.

The going was rough in the darkness and the rising wind. There would be a storm sometime tonight from the looks of the sky. It was possible, Carter thought, that if the storm did materialize, it would keep the natives from crossing to the other island for their attack.

He and Gabrielle only had to hold out until tomorrow morning when the *Starfish* was scheduled to arrive. Whatever was happening here on this island would be brought to an end.

Once they thought they could hear the cries of the natives somewhere far to the southwest, but then the wind gusted and a flash of lightning and crack of thunder made it impossible to tell for sure.

"It will rain tonight," Gabrielle said, looking up at the sky when they stopped for a rest.

Her neck was long and lovely. She was a beautiful woman. But Carter found himself wondering about her. There was something about her that was not quite right. Something he could not put his finger on.

"If the wind comes with it, the natives will not attack," he said.

She looked at him, a half smile on her lips. "You do not know these people. They have brought their outrigger canoes across the entire Pacific Ocean. In modern times they regularly go five hundred miles in all kinds of weather. A little local storm will not deter them, Nick. If anything, it will help cover their actions."

There it was again, Carter thought. Almost a pride in

what was happening here.

He had been leaning against a tree, smoking a cigarette. He straightened up now.

"Is there another holy ground, other than the volcano, here on the island?"

"I do not know," she said thoughtfully. "There may be. But I do not know of it." She looked into his eyes. "You mean the area around wherever the signal originated from?"

Carter nodded.

"It could very well be. But I doubt if we will ever find it."

"Why do you say that, Gabrielle?" Carter asked. He was becoming more and more uneasy with her.

"If it is nothing more than a little dish antenna, such as the one upon the hill, it would be like looking for a needle in the haystack. Impossible to find."

"You're right."

"We could spend days wandering around this island and never find a thing."

"You're right again, Gabrielle, except for one thing."

Her eyes narrowed. "What is that, Nick?"

"The helicopter was shot down, and the natives chased us up the hill. Now, this evening, their little show in the meeting place was interrupted. Whoever originated the signals knows we're here. They'll be looking for us. We've seen too much."

"So what if it is the Chinese?" she shouted. "This is French territory. We never wanted you or them here!"

"Then you know of the Chinese?"

"That is what I mean," Gabrielle snapped with irritation. "You tell me the equipment on the hill is of Chinese manufacture. It means they are here on this island. Your people are on Hiva Faui. We do not want either of you here. Look at the trouble you have caused for our people."

"But you've deserted your husband, Madame Rondine," Carter said, "or was that all a show just to find out what I was up to?"

She stamped her foot in frustration. "Do you suppose I came into your bed and made love with you just for information? Do you suppose I made up the story about my youth? A story that you could easily check?"

"I don't know, Gabrielle. I hope not, but I don't know."

"Bastard!" she hissed.

Carter looked at her for a long time. "I'm here to do a job," he said. "When it is finished you can return to the States with me or remain here. The choice will be yours. And if I am wrong about you, which I sincerely hope I am, then I apologize, Gabrielle. But I am paid to be a suspicious man. Many of my people have been killed. I have come to stop it. And I will."

"I too am sorry, Nick," Gabrielle said just a little too quickly. "I still have loyalties to France despite what has happened to me at the hands of Frenchmen . . . despite Albert. And I have a feeling for these poor people here."

"Then help me end the killing."

"I do not know if I can, Nick. How?"

"Help me find the Chinese installation here. The transmitting station where the pictures are sent to incite the natives."

"And then what? How can you stop them single-handedly?" Gabrielle asked, but then she stopped herself. "That is not it," she said. "You merely want to find out where the station is located and then you will call for help." She ran her fingers through her lovely dark hair. "My God, you want to start a war here on Natu Faui. Is that it? You crazy American."

"I want to stop a war," Carter said. "A war that began two years ago when the Chinese set up this operation."

"There will be fighting here!"

"Yes, but it will end the killing."

"The killing could end if your people left Hiva Faui!"

"The French would have to leave as well."

Gabrielle just looked at him.

"They wouldn't be satisfied merely to get rid of us. They'd want your people to leave as well."

"It is your spy satellite they want stopped . . ." Gabrielle said, but then she realized she had said too much.

Carter smiled sadly in the dim light. All along he had known something was wrong with her. All along he had suspected she was not telling him the truth.

She worked for the Chinese. Her husband probably did as well. It explained why there were so many Chinese workers on Hiva Faui, and it explained why the natives on this island were kept at barely above the primitive level. The natives acted as an effective buffer between the Chinese Communists and the Americans.

He did not think finding their base here would be very easy after all.

Gabrielle was looking at him, her eyes wide, her mouth pursed in an expression of contempt.

He reached out and grabbed for her arm, but she jumped back and reached for the .45 at her hip.

"Christ!" Carter swore. He dived left and scrambled into the thick undergrowth.

Gabrielle fired a shot well wide of its mark, and Carter lay flat on his stomach, watching her through the thick brush.

She was clearly frustrated and very upset. Evidently her assignment had been to keep tabs on Carter, and if he came too close or discovered too much, she was to kill him. She had failed.

Something made her turn away and cock her head as if she were listening for something. But Carter could not hear a thing.

She turned back and took several steps closer to the edge of the brush Carter had disappeared into, but then she shook her head in frustration.

"Nick," she called.

Carter remained still, watching her.

"If you are still out there and you can hear me, I want you to know that you will not get off this island alive." Again she looked over her shoulder as if she were listening for something.

She turned back.

"I want you to know that I am sorry it has to work out this way. I was not ordered to sleep with you . . . but I did it because I wanted to. You are a wonderful lover."

Once again she looked over her shoulder.

"I must go now, Nick. They will find you by morning. They never miss," she said.

She holstered her .45, then turned and headed off toward the north.

As soon as she was out of sight, Carter pushed himself up, emerged from the brush, and stopped long enough so that he could hear her up ahead.

TEN

Gabrielle moved quickly through the jungle. It was as if she knew exactly where she was going and had been on this path often. But Carter had no trouble following her in the darkness. Every ten or twenty yards he would stop and listen. He could hear her up ahead, crashing through the brush, making absolutely no effort to conceal herself.

It was several miles across to the north side of the island, and it took them better than an hour to make it.

Just like the north side of Hiva Faui, this island's north side rose up from the sea in high, sheer cliffs.

The jungle ended almost at the cliff's edge. Gabrielle was nowhere to be seen.

Carter hesitated just within the darkness of the trees. She had been just in front of him. He had lost the sounds of her progress because of the noise of the surf far below and the wind out of the northwest that was rising into a very stiff breeze that moaned around the rocks.

He was sure she had not turned parallel to the cliffs in order to keep to the cover of the jungle. He noticed some rocky hills to the east, and the jungle fell into a fairly deep valley a hundred yards to the west.

No, Carter decided, she had come this way. Which

118

meant there was a path down to the sea.

Keeping low, he stepped out from the jungle, crossed to the edge of the cliff, and looked over. Twenty or thirty yards to the west, and far below on the rocks, he just caught a glimpse of Gabrielle as she disappeared beneath a wide overhang.

There was a narrow stretch of beach farther west, and he waited, expecting to see her appear down there. But she did not. After a while he understood that she was either waiting down there somewhere beneath the overhang, or there was a passage within the cliff. He had a fair idea which it was.

He took out his Luger and worked his way along the cliff until he found the partly natural and partly man-made path, and he started down.

A hundred feet below, the sea moved in huge swells into what appeared to be one of the larger natural caves cut into the face of the cliff. The path he was on crossed over the top of the cave, then came down on the western edge where it twisted around beneath the over-hang.

Just before he eased around the corner, which would put him in full view of the cave, Carter hesitated and listened.

At first he heard nothing, but then he thought he heard a snatch of conversation over the roar of the surf.

He moved a little closer, crouched down, and listened again. He heard a voice. There was definitely someone around the edge. Talking. In Chinese.

This was evidently the entrance to the Chinese base. It explained to Carter why the previous naval shore parties here had failed to turn up anything other than natives and native villages. Before they arrived, the dish antennae had been taken down, and there would be nothing topside to indicate that a base was located here.

Carter turned and started back up the path, holstering his Luger. He would hike farther west now, down into the valley and around the island on the beaches if need be, until he found an outrigger. When the storm abated in the morning, he would take off for Hiva Faui. The *Starfish* would be there by then, and they could come back here and close this place down. Afterward the governor and his wife would be arrested and shipped back to Paris for trial.

Halfway up the path someone above shouted something in Chinese, and several other men laughed.

Carter froze where he was. Below, around the twist that led beneath the overhang, were a couple of guards. Above, boxing him in, were are least three or four men.

He figured he could probably take them out, but then whatever element of surprise he would have tomorrow would be gone. They would know he had been here. They would know he had discovered the entrance to their installation.

The patrol above was nearly to the path when Carter finally accepted his only alternative. He looked over the edge, down fifty or sixty feet to the big swells roaring like freight trains into the cave. It would be hell swimming back out of there, if swimming were possible. But it would be better than remaining where he was.

Someone above shouted something else—it sounded like a joke—and the others laughed uproariously as Carter shook his head, then stepped cleanly away from the path, his body plummeting toward the dark water below.

As he fell he tried to listen for any sounds of an alarm from above, but then he hit the water cleanly at the trough of a swell, plunging deeply, the sea surprisingly warm. He could feel the powerful current pushing his body into the cave as he fought his way back to the surface.

Then he was clear, and he took deep breaths of the warm, moist air, the incoming swell shoving him up and farther inside the wide cavern.

Twenty yards away and less than ten feet above the surface of the water within the cavern was a catwalk. Carter was being shoved past two guards leaning over the rail and smoking cigarettes as they stared at the water. They would see him!

He sank beneath the surface of the water and struggled out of his boots, then swam with the current, his strokes powerful.

When he came to the surface, he was well past the guards and even the catwalk. Here the ceiling of the cave sloped abruptly down to the water, so that each swell that crashed in from the open sea threatened to smash Carter against the rocks. He could feel the current tugging against his body, pulling him down and toward the inner wall when it should have been rebounding and shoving him back out toward the opening.

He managed to swim to one side of the cave and clung to the rocks.

Several yards from the front of the cave the catwalk ended. There was a doorway, and Carter supposed it led back into the hillside.

He stopped and held his breath, suddenly conscious of a low-pitched hum, more like a deep-throated vibration, through the rocks and the water. Was that what Gabrielle had been listening for? Even from miles away? Then he remembered the rhythmic rumblings he had heard with Tieggs from the helicopter.

There was something . . . some machinery just on the other side of the wall forming the back of the cave. That was why the current was acting the way it was. There was another way inside, Carter realized. By water.

As soon as he felt he was rested enough, he swam

back out to the middle of the cave, the current very strong there.

If the underwater passage was too long, or if it branched off, he would be dead, he realized. There would be no swimming against this current until the tide changed. From what he was able to see from where he swam, the tide was still coming up. He could see shells, algae, and other growth another foot or so up the cave walls.

But there had been a lot of good people killed on these islands over the past couple of years. And this was his job.

He took several deep breaths, held one, and dived deep, swimming as strongly as he could with the current toward the back of the cave.

The current became much stronger at one point, propelling him very fast beneath an opening in the back wall of the cave. There definitely would be no turning back now, he thought.

He had the impression that the water was very deep beneath him and that the opening was very wide.

His heart was pounding in his ears and his lungs were beginning to ache when he saw a glow through the water ahead and above him.

He angled upward toward it, forcing himself to slow down so that when he broke the surface of the water it would not be with a splash.

His head broke the surface, and he took in great lungsful of air, his mouth wide so that he would make as little noise as possible.

He had started to sink back into the water when he suddenly focused on two huge shapes floating at the far end of the cave, both of them bathed in lights and swarming with uniformed men.

Two nuclear submarines were tied to a long cement dock, the big gold star faced by the four smaller gold stars of Communist China painted on the sides.

One of the submarines was being unloaded. A growing stack of crates was piling up on the dock as two cranes pulled what probably were supplies for this base from the hold of the sub.

It explained the secrecy. Somehow the Chinese had discovered a natural cavern here in the rocks. Coming in with their construction equipment and supplies, they had built this place.

Either that, Carter thought, carefully treading water as he caught his breath, or it had been a Japanese installation during World War II. Possibly a sub pen.

The gallery he was in was very long in comparison to its width. He was facing the subs bow on. They had evidently come in here bow first and then had been warped around so that they faced out again.

There was nothing to the left. To the right there was only a single narrow catwalk that led, presumably through some passage through the rocks, to the outer cave. Somehow the catwalk in the outer cave would have to be concealed, Carter reasoned, so that the natives did not stumble on it.

At the far end of the gallery, beyond where the subs were being unloaded, was a large glassed-in area above the level of the docks. It looked like some sort of a control booth. Evidently the subs' operations were directed from there. Directly in front of the glassed-in area was a long balcony upon which several uniformed men were lounging.

Even at this distance something seemed odd about their dress.

This base was evidently much more than a simple Communist Chinese installation to harass a U.S. spy satellite receiving station. It was a nuclear submarine hideout.

The Soviets had them, as did the U.S. Navy. There were spots all around the globe where nuclear submarines could hide from the increasingly sophisticated detection systems that each government maintained.

Had the location of this Chinese sub base been known, the problem of the harassment of U.S. personnel on Hiva Faui would have been stopped by a simple diplomatic message.

It was likely, Carter figured, that the Chinese had had this as a secret base of operations long before the satellite tracking and receiving station was put up.

And yet he had to wonder why they would risk discovery of this place just to force the closure of a receiving station. The information the Hiva Faui station was gathering from the spy satellite must have been devastating to the Chinese for them to risk so much.

Very slowly, very carefully, using a gentle breaststroke, Carter swam toward the submarines. There were so many lights on the boats and illuminating the dock area that unless he came too close, no one topside would be able to see him. The entire area of the water was in relative darkness.

The soldiers on the balcony were dressed, Carter could see now, in some sort of khaki uniforms with sloping caps from which neck cloths were attached. Rifles leaned up against the railing.

A little closer and it suddenly came to him. They were dressed as World War II Japanese soldiers!

They were probably the troops who patrolled the islands. If the natives encountered them, after all that had happened here on this island, they would believe they had another religious experience. They would believe they had seen men from forty years ago!

The light show that the natives were fed, apparently on a regular basis, probably supported this belief as well.

It was a very sophisticated setup, Carter decided. This base was probably Communist China's major refueling and resupply point for her Pacific nuclear submarine pack.

He slowly worked his way around the outer submarine, keeping the bulbous hull of the huge boat
between himself and the dock. The only way anyone
would spot him there would be if a crewman decided
to take a stroll on the deck and look down. Not likely,
he figured.

When he came close enough, he reached out and
touched the side of the boat. He could feel the hum of
machinery through the hull. The boat was alive. He put
his ear to the outer hull and could hear an amalgam of
sounds, at one point even the sound of someone shouting something.

The tide was still coming in; its current had driven
him inside. Carter figured it would be at least another
half hour or forty-five minutes before it was slack tide
and he would have any chance of swimming out of
there. Meanwhile, he was going to have to make sure
he was not detected. And he was going to have to be out
of the way in case one or both of the subs had orders to
sail. If he was caught swimming this close, he would
be sucked down with the boat.

Quietly he worked his way along the length of the
sub, coming to the stern, beyond which the dock ex-
tended farther back into the darkness.

He swam the rest of the way to the back of the
cavern, angling toward the dock, and the water on the
floor of the cavern suddenly got so shallow he could
stand. Rocks were piled up against the cavern walls,
and at one spot the rocks met the end of the concrete
dock area.

Carefully Carter scrambled up to the dock and
crouched in the darkness as he watched the activity
around the submarines at least fifty yards away.

The unloading activity around the aft submarine
continued, but as Carter watched, a dozen men came
out onto the balcony above, said something to the
soldiers, then tromped down the stairs and across the
dock to the forward submarine.

Several of the men appeared to be officers, and as other crewmen emerged from the sub, the officers issued a string of orders.

Hatches were closed, and electrical and water lines connecting the boat to the dock were removed and coiled. The submarine was being made ready to depart.

All hell would break loose, Carter realized, if the presence of the *Starfish* in these waters was detected. He did not think there would be a fight. But the Chinese would definitely be pressed to do everything within their power to divert the American sub from discovering this place.

Several other people from inside the base came out onto the balcony and started down the stairs. One of them was Gabrielle. Carter recognized her slight form from where he crouched, and he stiffened.

Any lingering doubts he had that she had stumbled accidentally on this place, or that she was a captive, dissipated as he watched her come across the dock and shake the hands of the officers by the sub.

She was shown aboard and helped down one of the hatches. Within the next few minutes the final preparations for departure were finished, and the crew and officers clambered aboard, the hatches were closed, and a siren sounded a brief warning.

The sub, no longer attached to the dock, had begun to drift toward the back of the cavern, but suddenly it eased away from the dock toward the center of the cavern and slowly sank out of sight as it moved forward toward the front wall. Then it was gone, leaving behind only a few ripples in its wake.

Gabrielle was aboard. If the sub was on a war mission, or if it was heading out to divert the *Starfish*, they would never allow a civilian aboard. They were taking her somewhere. Possibly to a rendezvous with a boat from Hiva Faui.

Several other soldiers came from the glassed-in control area, and they also walked down the stairs to the dock. They slung their rifles over their shoulders and quick-stepped along the dock to the door that led to the catwalk in the outer cavern.

Carter figured they would be going out to look for the American who had come with Gabrielle and who had upset the natives. He didn't think Gabrielle knew that he had gotten to the cliffs. She had probably told them to begin their search well inland.

The unloading of the other submarine was still going on an hour later when Carter, who had remained hidden in the darkness at the end of the dock, slipped back into the warm tropical water and swam toward the underground passage to the open sea.

The tide was at slack; there was no longer any current to move the water. He would not have to fight against it on the way out, but there would be no ebbing flow to help him either.

At the end of the cavern, Carter treaded water for a few minutes to catch his breath. He watched the Chinese soldiers unloading the sub. There were a lot of supplies piled up on the dock already. A huge pile, in fact. Enough to supply a large contingent of men. He suddenly got the uncomfortable feeling that this installation was a hell of a lot bigger than he first suspected it was.

He took several deep breaths in quick succession, hyperventilating slightly, then plunged powerfully down through the pitch-black water. This time there were no lights at the other side to guide him upward. He swam as rapidly as he could, his heart exploding in his chest, his lungs screaming for oxygen, until finally he started upward in a long curve.

He broke the surface of the water about five yards beyond the rock wall. There were no soldiers on the catwalk above, but even if there had been, they would

not have been able to hear Carter's gasps for air over
the noise of the wind and crashing waves.

Cautiously he swam toward the entrance of the
cavern. The wind had shifted in the hour or so he had
been inside, and now the waves did not roar directly
into the cavern. But just outside he could hear the surf
crashing angrily against the rocks.

There would be absolutely no way for him to survive
swimming out there. He would be instantly dashed
against the rocks and killed.

He quickly swam to the side of the cavern, then
scrambled up on the rocks, over the rail, and onto the
catwalk. The walkway was damp with moisture, so he
would leave no wet footprints for someone to discover.

He took out his stiletto and hurried along the catwalk
to where it ended fifty or sixty feet from the mouth of
the cavern. From there he picked his way along a
well-concealed path to the outside, where he crouched
down and looked around.

The sea was wild. There was no rain yet, but in the
distance there was thunder and lightning as the storm
developed toward Hiva Faui. It could be hours before it
developed its full strength. He was going to have to
beat that storm to Hiva Faui.

Outside, there were no guards at the overhang nor
did he see any on the path above. They had apparently
joined the patrol that had been sent out to look for him.

He quickly made his way up the path to the top of the
cliffs. The wind was becoming quite strong now out of
the west. It was not going to be easy to get back to the
other island. If he could make it at all.

He picked his way down the steep incline to the
west, then headed up the island parallel to the rocks
along the shoreline.

Within an hour Carter had reached the end of the
cliff area, and the rocks gave way to the wide sand
beach. After a half hour's walk, he came upon the

outriggers pulled well above the beach and tied to palm trees.

He ducked back into the protection of the jungle as he watched for any sign that the natives had posted guards. There were none. Somewhere inland, probably not too far, was one of the native villages.

The waves marched onto the beach at an angle from the west. If he could get the outrigger past the breakers, Carter figured he would have at least a chance to make it over to Hiva Faui.

Carter picked out one of the smaller outriggers, designed for only four or five men, cut it loose from the trees, found a couple of paddles, and dragged the boat down to the crashing waves.

The canoe was surprisingly light and flimsy, but it seemed to handle the water very well as he waded into the first breaker.

He was shoved off his feet and almost lost his grip on the canoe, but then he scrambled back up, pushing the boat ahead of him before the next wave hit, knocking him over.

By degrees he finally managed to get the canoe into chest-deep water. After the next wave he flopped into the boat, and despite his exhaustion, he paddled as fast as he possibly could.

The next gigantic wave nearly flipped him up and over, but then he was roaring down the back of the wave as the next breaker began looming above him.

The little outrigger rose to meet this wave, and Carter got to the other side of it easily, heading—as best he could figure—directly north toward Hiva Faui as the storm deepened.

ELEVEN

Throughout the night the wind kept shifting counterclockwise from the west and finally from the south. Nick Carter had been blown far to the east of his intended course, but as the wind shifted he was better able to make headway, finally rocketing to the north toward Hiva Faui.

Most of the time he could not see the waves, but whenever a flash of lightning would light up the sky, he would catch a glimpse of mountainous waves that towered far above him, momentarily blocking the strong wind.

The little outrigger canoe was never in any serious danger, Carter decided early in the evening. It was very uncomfortable, bouncing up and down with the waves, and it was very wet, but there never seemed to be any danger of the boat breaking apart and going down. The natives had designed their boats for these waters, and they had designed them well.

Carter did a lot of thinking about Gabrielle, and he decided that the story about her background was probably true. She was not a good enough actress to have convinced him of it if the story were not true. But he suspected that Governor Rondine had some other hold on her as well. Something that made her do whatever it was she was told.

He also did a lot of thinking about the Chinese base on Natu Faui and the U.S. satellite tracking and receiving station on Hiva Faui. Two countries were both in this part of the world for the same reasons: the U.S. because from here they could easily spy on the Chinese, and the Chinese because from these islands they commanded the entire western Pacific basin—from Japan to Australia—with their submarines.

At times Carter paddled hard, and it seemed as if he made headway. But mostly he just lay back in the canoe and let the wind and waves propel him to the north.

He actually dozed off a few times during the night, and he found that he had gone from pitch-black to a dull, dirty gray with no real awareness of the passage of time.

He sat up and shivered. He was soaked to the skin and very cold even though the air temperature had to be in the mid- to high seventies.

It was dawn, and although the rain had stopped for the moment, the sky was still heavily overcast. The wind was blowing with much more force than it had been when Carter left Natu Faui.

Dead ahead about two or three miles, the surf was breaking on the beach of a large island. Hiva Faui, Carter hoped, but he was not at all sure. It looked like any other island, except for Natu Faui with its distinctive volcano.

If it was Hiva Faui, he suspected he was somewhere mid-island. Coming up on it from the south, the satellite station would be to the west, and the town of Hiva Faui would be to the right, to the east.

He picked up one of the paddles and began angling the outrigger to the east. From time to time he looked at his watch. It was nearing seven o'clock. The *Starfish* was due at the public docks at any time now. He wanted to be there when the governor was summoned to the docks. He wanted to see what the man was going to do. He also wanted to see what Gabrielle's reaction would be . . . if she had been brought back.

There was much more to this business, Carter suspected, than met the eye. The Chinese maintained a base on Natu Faui, but he believed it was with the knowledge and cooperation of Governor Rondine. He did not think very much happened on these islands without the governor's knowledge.

Sooner or later, he knew he was going to have to deal with the governor and the man's organization. There had been plenty of muscle visible at the party. And most of the people who had arrived from the other islands in this part of the Pacific were probably just as involved in their own schemes on other islands. They would have to be dealt with eventually as well.

The canoe, headed at an angle to the very large waves, would ride up over the top of one, its outrigger in midair at times. Then the canoe would tip to the down side and race down the front of the wave, burying its nose momentarily in the trough. Then it would start up the next one.

Slowly Carter angled the canoe farther and farther down the island, finally rounding a headland that gave protection to the harbor of the town.

Even from outside the breakwater Carter could see the sail of the *Starfish* alongside the long public docks. It seemed as if there were a lot of people on the dock and in the square. There seemed to be a lot of cars parked along the main road.

Carter redoubled his efforts, sending the outrigger up and over the last few large waves before he shot through the breakwater and into the protection of the inner harbor.

Lightning flashed to the south and west, and moments later it began to pour, the rain coming down so hard it flattened the waves outside the breakwater and obliterated Carter's view of everything more than a few yards away.

He kept pushing, stroke after stroke, the paddle biting deeply and cleanly into the water, propelling the lightweight canoe through the water so fast it created a substantial bow wave. Carter felt that he was using up what small amounts of reserve strength he had left, but it was absolutely essential that the commander of the *Starfish* understand what he was up against before he turned back out to sea to face the Chinese subs.

There was no telling what the on-board surveillance equipment had picked up already, or what Governor Rondine was telling the commander.

The rain lessened momentarily. It was long enough for Carter to see that a lot of people had left the dock, but others had opened umbrellas and remained.

The *Starfish* was still there. There were crewmen on the deck. Carter could make them out from where he was.

He stopped long enough to raise his paddle and swing it back and forth over his head, but then the rain intensified, and he went back to his paddling.

The rain slowed down again for a time when Carter was still a couple of hundred yards from the dock, and someone aboard the sub spotted him.

Within a minute or so an inflatable was brought up on deck, shoved in the water, and an outboard motor was attached. Four crewmen climbed aboard, and they headed out to him. Carter stopped paddling.

When they were just a few yards away, the crewman operating the motor swore out loud and cut the engine.

"Good morning," Carter said.

"Holy shit," the crewman said again. "Mr. Carter?"

"Right," Carter said. The inflatable had drifted

closer. One of the crewmen tossed Carter a line that he made fast at the bow of the canoe.

"They said you may have gone down in the crash of a chopper on one of the other islands, sir," the petty officer said.

"I wasn't aboard," Carter called. "Get me back. I have to talk with your skipper."

"Aye-aye, sir," the crewman said, and he started the inflatable's motor, turned back toward the sub, and headed out, the outrigger pulled along behind.

There were a half-dozen crewmen on the deck of the sub and several officers on the dock with about three or four dozen civilians.

Carter immediately recognized Governor Rondine in the midst of the group, several burly-looking men holding large umbrellas over him.

Gabrielle was nowhere to be seen in the group, but as they came up to the sub, so that Carter was in clear view of everyone on the dock, the governor nodded. One of his people hurried back to the road, where he got in one of the cars and took off. As the car turned the corner toward the square, Carter was certain he caught a glimpse of Gabrielle in the back seat.

Carter scrambled aboard the submarine just as a tall, well-built man in his late forties or early fifties came from the dock and around the sail.

"Mr. Carter?" he asked.

Carter nodded, and they shook hands.

"I'm Captain Don Petti. We were told that you may have crashed aboard a helicopter on the island of Natu Faui."

"The chief of security for the receiver station, Richard Fenster, was killed. I wasn't aboard."

Captain Petti glanced down at the frail outrigger, then back at Carter. "You came across in *that*? Last night?"

"Right," Carter said. "But there isn't a whole hell

of a lot of time left us. I'm going to need your complete cooperation for the next twenty-four hours, Captain.''

"You got it, Carter. My orders were to assist you in any way possible. They came from the Joint Chiefs themselves.''

"Good,'' Carter said. "First of all, I want you to invite the island's governor aboard and down to the wardroom.''

"Can do.''

"I'm going to say some things down there that aren't completely true. I want you to go along with me. Tell your officers the same thing.''

"Are you going to tell me what's really going on?'' the captain asked, his right eyebrow raising.

"As soon as we get rid of the governor, you'll get a full briefing. And believe me, it's damned important, and time is critical.''

"Right,'' the captain said. He turned to one of his crewmen. "Take Mr. Carter below to the officer's wardroom. Make sure we have coffee. Get him something warm and dry to wear. And have Mr. Patterson and his people assemble on the double.''

"Aye-aye, sir,'' the crewman said, and Carter followed him belowdecks as Captain Petti went back around to the dock to invite Governor Rondine aboard.

Down two levels, the crewman led Carter aft and then into a large, tastefully furnished wardroom. There were a lot of crewmen hurrying back and forth throughout the boat. They would be hurrying even more as soon as their officers were briefed, Carter thought.

"Mr. Patterson, Mr. Patterson, to the wardroom on the double, with section red,'' the crewman spoke into the ship's intercom.

Section red aboard the sub referred to its intelligence gathering section. Carter figured that Patterson was probably the section chief.

The crewman, whose name tag said MacPherson, poured Carter a cup of coffee. "Be right back, sir, with a change of clothing."

"Just bring me a towel, MacPherson," Carter said. "Stand by on the change of clothes."

"Yes, sir," the man said, and he left the wardroom.

He was back a moment or two later with a large bath towel. "Dungarees okay, sir?"

"That'll be fine as soon as we're done in here."

"Yes, sir," the crewman said and left.

Captain Petti appeared in the doorway, and he motioned for someone else to enter first. Governor Rondine stepped into view, his eyes locking with Carter's, and then he walked inside, his impressive bulk seeming to fill the room.

Captain Petti and a half-dozen other officers all filed in as well, and when they were seated, a steward came in and poured them all coffee.

"We thought you were dead, Mr. Carter," the governor said dryly in English.

"I was lucky," Carter said. "But I'm afraid I have some bad news for you."

The governor waited.

"Your wife came with us to Natu-Faui. I lost her in the jungle. She's probably still there."

The governor ponderously shook his head. "Like you she braved the storm aboard one of the native outriggers. She was rescued this morning less than a half hour before this warship showed up." The governor turned to Captain Petti. "And I will restate my demand, Captain, that this vessel be removed immediately from French territorial waters."

Captain Petti smiled graciously. "I am sorry, sir, but that will not be possible for just a few hours. We have orders to come here on an inspection tour of our installation. The treaty between our governments allows for such inspection tours."

"By aircraft."

"The mode of transportation, I believe, has not been specified, sir."

The governor was about to protest further, but Carter interrupted him.

"You don't understand, Governor, but there is serious trouble on Natu Faui."

The governor turned to Carter.

"Our helicopter didn't just crash. It was shot down."

For a moment the governor's expression did not change, but finally he laughed. "By the natives? With bow and arrow? An incredibly lucky shot."

"No, sir, not by the natives. By some kind of a rocket or perhaps a bazooka."

"The natives do not have such weapons, Mr. Carter."

"No, they don't," Carter said. He turned to the captain and the sub's officers, and he quickly explained what had happened with the helicopter, then about the light show, and finally about the antenna. But he did not tell them that he had followed Gabrielle to the sub pen entrance, nor did he tell them that he had swum into the cavern.

"That's incredible," Captain Petti said.

Governor Rondine was eyeing Carter. "What are you saying, Carter? That someone is inciting the natives to riot against your people?"

"Yes."

"Who?"

"There were Chinese characters on the dish antenna. I saw them clearly."

Captain Petti sat forward at that. "The Chinese? Communist Chinese?"

"I don't know who else, Captain," Carter said. "It's not likely they'd have a base on the island. We'd have known about it by now. It was a dish antenna. I'm sure the signals are sent to the island by satellite.''

"What are you suggesting we do about it, Carter?''
the captain asked.

''I want to go over there this morning, take a party
inland, and dismantle the antenna and the receiving
equipment at the amphitheater.''

Captain Petti nodded. He turned to Governor Rondine, who was looking just a little smug. "It's French
territory, Governor. Do we have your permission to
operate such a mission, or should we go through diplomatic channels?''

"You have my permission, Captain. In fact I will
join you there. I will come over by helicopter as an
observer. If there is, as Mr. Carter suggests, Chinese
equipment on Natu Faui, I want to know about it, and I
want it destroyed. A formal complaint will be lodged at
the U.N. as well, I assure you.''

"Fine," Captain Petti said, standing. "Then we can
get underway within . . . two hours, shall we say?''

The governor had gotten to his feet. "We will watch
for you, Captain." he said. "When you pull out we
will head over to the island.''

"Very good, Governor," the captain said, and he
detailed one of his people to show the governor off the
boat.

MacPherson came back. "I have your dry clothing,
sir," he said to Carter and handed over a pair of jeans.

When he was gone Carter got up and motioned for
the door to be closed as he unbuttoned his soggy shirt.

"We have an extremely serious situation on our
hands here, gentlemen," Carter said, pulling off his
shirt. He unstrapped his stiletto and his Luger, and laid
the weapons on the table.

"What's the actual situation over there, Carter?''
the captain asked.

"What I told Rondine was essentially correct, as far
as it went, but not only is there Chinese equipment on

that island, there is a Communist base. A submarine pen.''

"Jesus," one of the officers swore.

"We're going to have to get some kind of authorization even to be here," the captain said. "We can't mess with a possible confrontation.''

"Send a radio signal out of here, and they'll know that I discovered their base. But there'll be a confrontation in any event. One of their subs left the pen late last night.''

"It's out, on the loose? Nearby?"

"Presumably," Carter said.

"Damn," Petti said, running his fingers through his gray hair. He looked up at Carter. "You'd better start at the beginning, Mr. Carter, and give me every bit of it, and then tell me what you want us to do. I'll have to decide whether or not this vessel can handle it.''

One of the officers got up, went to a sideboard, and brought back a bottle of bourbon. He poured a measure of it into his coffee, then passed the bottle around.

Carter went over everything that had happened to him from the moment he had arrived on Hiva Faui until he was picked up by the crewmen with the inflatable.

When he was finished, the officers were all silent for a long time. Captain Petti finally spoke up.

"I'd like to ask if you're absolutely sure of your facts. But it's your business to be sure. And besides, you can't mistake a pair of Red Chinese subs in an island cavern.''

"No," Carter said, drying off and then getting dressed. "I need some oil and a rag.''

One of the officers went out to get the things. Carter sat down and began taking apart Wilhelmina. The Luger had been in salt water for a long time.

"You evidently have a plan in mind," Captain Petti said.

Carter nodded.

"I almost hate to ask what it is," the captain said. "But before we get started I want you to understand that my orders do not include compromising this boat. If and when it comes to a standoff between us and the Chinese subs, I will have to have further authority. If I can't get it, we will have to get out of here. They are not our waters."

"By the time that occurs, we will have done what was needed."

Carter had finished cleaning his weapons, and Captain Petti was busy getting his boat and crew ready for the operation on Natu Faui, when Justin Owen and Bob Tieggs showed up on the dock.

The first officer, Lt. Ashcroft, was just going up to talk to them when Carter came out of the wardroom. He went up with the man.

They were both shocked to see Carter, and they hurried across to him.

"Christ, they said you were probably dead," Tieggs said, pounding Carter on the back.

"Fenster was killed."

"That's what the governor told us," Owen said. "But we thought you had gone down too. They were going to send someone over this morning as soon as the weather calmed down."

"The bastards sabotaged our other chopper," Tieggs said bitterly. "Otherwise I would have been over there and back by now."

Owen had turned to the first officer. "I'd like to speak with the captain."

"Captain Petti sends his regrets, sir, but we are making ready to sail, and he is extremely busy."

"Don't worry about it," Carter said. "We're going to take care of the problem."

"I'd like to come along," Tieggs said.

"I'm sorry, sir, but that won't be possible," Lt.

Ashcroft said before Carter could speak.

"Goddamnit, Nick, I want to come along!" Tieggs insisted.

"It's not your job, Bob," Carter said gently. "But there is something else you can do for me."

"Goddamnit . . ."

Carter led Tieggs away, well out of earshot of the other two men. "Now listen to me, Bob. We're going over there this morning to take care of it. It's not something you can do, nor is it something you could help with. But the governor is involved in this up to his ears. I think there's a very good chance he's working for the Chinese Communists."

"The Chinese Com—?"

"That's right. His wife may be working for them as well."

Tieggs did not want to believe it.

"She was with me over there. But I think she's back here. The governor and some of his people are going to fly over to the island this morning. While they're gone, I want you to snoop around. See if his wife is still here."

"I don't understand any of this," Tieggs said. "But I'll do as you say, Nick."

"But be careful, Bob," Carter said. "These people are not fooling around."

TWELVE

It was close to eleven in the morning by the time the *Starfish* slipped her dock lines and moved out toward the breakwater protecting the Hiva Faui harbor. The wind had calmed considerably, although the sky was still heavily overcast, and occasionally it would rain very hard for a few minutes, cutting visibility to near zero.

Nick Carter had gone over, in great detail, exactly what he wanted to do. Captain Petti agreed in principle, with one caution.

"We're going to be watching for the other sub," he said.

"I understand," Carter said, looking up from the sketch of the sub pen he had drawn.

They were gathered in the situation room just below the bridge in the conning tower. They were on red operational lights. Everyone looked like a Halloween ghoul.

"If they show up, or if the sub you say was unloading in the pen comes out, we're bugging out. We'll have to stand by until we can get some definitive orders one way or the other."

"I understand that too, Captain," Carter said. "Just get me there. I'll do the rest."

Carter's plan had been a simple one. They would approach the island from the sub pen side. Carter, wearing scuba gear, would slip out of the *Starfish* from an underwater hatch. With him he would carry enough explosives to destroy the sub inside the pen and hopefully the cavern itself. Meanwhile, the *Starfish* would proceed to the far side of the island where a shore party would go inland to seek out and destroy the dish antenna and the projection equipment in the amphitheater. Carter had pinpointed both sites on a chart.

A burly lieutenant who had been standing in the background stepped forward. His voice matched his appearance.

"Begging the captain's pardon, but my people are ready. We would like to go on this with Mr. Carter."

Carter looked at him. His name was Jakes. "I'm taking no one with me, Lieutenant."

"Begging your pardon, sir. But aboard this boat that's not your decision. Besides, you couldn't carry enough explosives to be one-hundred-percent certain you'd destroy their operation."

Captain Petti looked at him. "You understand we might have to leave you, Paul?"

"Aye-aye, sir."

"How about your people? Any volunteers?"

Jakes grinned. "Hell, sir, we had to draw lots to see who'd come with me . . . there'll only be one other. It was the only way I could hold down the fights. They all wanted in on it."

"Carter?" the captain said, looking at Carter. He was giving him a choice.

Carter turned to the lieutenant. "Can you swim?"

"A little, sir," Jakes said, his grin widening.

"I can't, so I'd better have you along."

"Yes, sir!"

They did not bother submerging for the short trip across to Natu Faui, nor did they run at their full speed of nearly sixty knots. Officially they were only capable of forty-five knots, and they kept to that speed.

Carter described the area to the west of the cavern where he had picked up the outrigger canoe. If all went well, the *Starfish* would rendezvous there exactly ninety minutes from the time Carter, Jakes, and his one crewman entered the water. They would all be working on a very tight timetable. Less could go wrong that way.

"This is incredible, Carter," Captain Petti said. "But not surprising, considering everything else that's been happening lately."

"And that's just the half of it," Carter said not unkindly.

"I know. Good luck."

"Thanks."

Carter went with Jakes below to the UDT operations room, where he was introduced to a wiry kid from Minnesota who knew all there was to know about demolitions. His name was Arte Haikkinen, third-generation Finnish.

They donned their wet suits and scuba gear, and Jakes explained the operation of the demolitions they would carry, as well as the operation of the wet room from which they would be leaving the sub.

"On our signal, the captain will order the boat slowed, but there'll still be a hell of a current. Go with it. Don't even try to fight it. You might wind up with a broken back."

"They'll be watching us pretty closely," Haikkinen volunteered.

"Right. As we pass by the opening to their sub pen, they'll be watching us real close. We're getting off a mile before that."

"Any questions, or are we all straight?" Jakes asked.

"Are we going to stand here and talk about it, or are we going?" Carter asked.

They checked each other's gear, strapped on the explosives, and the amber light over the wet room flicked on. Jakes picked up the phone. "We're ready," he said, then hung up.

They entered the wet room, which was not much larger than a telephone booth, dogged the hatch, and flooded it. The bottom hatch dropped open automatically, but Jakes held them from going until the amber light above the door flicked to green, then he shoved Haikkinen down.

Before he could turn around, Carter shoved himself powerfully through the hatch. He had done this more than once before, so he was prepared for the tremendous shock of the very fast current that instantly swept him down and away from the sub.

Within a few moments Jakes was overhead, and Haikkinen was at his side. They made sure they were all right, then headed off to the east, the submarine already far out of sight.

The water was warm. They were at about forty feet, so they were far below the wind and waves on the surface. And although he was tired, Carter found himself falling into an easy, relaxed rhythm that seemed effortless yet ate up the distance.

They closed with the shore and allowed the incoming tide to help them along, finally coming to what appeared to be the opening to the cavern.

Carter motioned for Jakes and Haikkinen to remain submerged while he rose to the surface well within the cavern.

His head broke the surface, and he was looking directly into the eyes of a man standing on the catwalk. Carter didn't move, and a second or two later the soldier flipped his cigarette into the water and turned around. He had not seen a thing!

Slowly Carter let a little air out of his buoyancy control vest, and he sank beneath the surface. They were in the right cavern. Jakes's navigation had been perfect.

It was much deeper in the channel that ran into the center of the sub pen. At one point they were seventy-five feet down, and still they had not reached the bottom.

They started up after Carter felt they were well beneath the wall and probably a bit to the west.

Twenty feet from the surface they could see lights above, and a little farther to the west, the hulk of the submarine.

Carter stopped Jakes and Haikkinen and pointed toward the sub. They both nodded.

Quickly they angled upward until they were directly beneath the keel of the huge nuclear sub. Jakes motioned for them to remain where they were, and he worked his way aft to the rudders.

A minute or so later Jakes was back. He did not have his pack of explosives with him. Haikkinen worked his way forward and up the side of the hull to a series of what appeared to be vents. They were probably in the vicinity of the sub's nuclear reactor. After the explosion, whether or not the cavern was destroyed, it would be radioactive for years to come.

He attached the package of high explosives to the side of the sub, swam back to Carter and Jakes, then they all headed back to the bow, where they slowly and carefully surfaced.

The mound of supplies that had been piled on the dock was gone. There were no soldiers in sight. Only the harsh overhead lights illuminated the scene.

The installation was probably on alert because of the presence of the U.S. submarine. The troops would all be at battle stations.

Carter suspected the only ways out of this place were by submarine or through the passageway to the catwalk and from there to the cliffs.

He thought about the young Chinese men manning their electronic surveillance instruments deep within the bowels of the hillside. When the sub blew out here, they wouldn't have a chance.

But then they had not given the natives a chance. Nor had they shown any mercy to the civilian employees at the satellite receiving station on Hiva Faui.

"What's the matter, Carter?" Jakes asked.

"Wait here," Carter said, and he swam around the bow, wriggled out of his scuba gear, and climbed up on the dock.

"Carter . . . Carter . . . get back here," Jakes whispered urgently.

Carter looked down at him. "Give me five minutes. If I'm not back by then, get the hell out of here."

He slung the explosives over his shoulder, and with his Luger in hand he crossed the dock and scrambled up the stairs that led to the operations room.

At the top he kept low, below the level of the large plate glass windows, until he made it to the door.

Carefully he straightened up so that he could just see inside the room. There were several consoles of electronic equipment along one wall, and along the other were a couch and chairs, and a couple of tables. But there was no one inside.

Carter got up, opened the door, and slipped inside.

It was very quiet in the room. He stood for several moments holding his breath, listening to the sounds of running machinery elsewhere in the installation.

There was a noise outside on the steps. Carter spun around and dropped below the windows, the safety of his Luger off.

He was pressed up against the wall a few feet away

from the door. If anyone came through, he would have a clear shot.

The door opened slightly, and a second later Jakes slipped into the room. Carter almost shot him before he realized who it was. A moment later Haikkinen came in.

Jakes had started to turn when he saw Carter crouched against the wall.

"Christ," he whispered.

Carter got up. Both men had gotten rid of their scuba gear. Jakes was armed with a .45 automatic, as was Haikkinen. They had not planned on surfacing, so had not brought anything other than handguns with them.

"What the hell are you doing here, Jakes?"

"I might ask you the same, sir. But I think I know."

"Then get the hell out of here."

"We're in this together, sir," Haikkinen said. "Besides, I'd just as soon place the charges. I think I might be able to do a better job."

Carter handed over the satchel, then looked at his watch. It was a little past 12:30. They had less than twenty minutes to finish here and get away before the charges on the sub went off.

"Along the west side of the dock there's a catwalk that leads to the outside. There's a guard there . . . I saw only one, but there may be others. There's a path up the cliff face. From there you can get inland and back to the west to the beach."

Jakes and Haikkinen both nodded. Carter turned and hurried across the room to a door set between two equipment consoles.

Before he eased the door open, he stuck his Luger into the waistband of his wet suit and pulled out his stiletto and a small gas bomb.

A soldier stood just on the other side. Carter eased the door closed, motioned for Jakes and Haikkinen to stand aside, then knocked on the door.

A moment later it opened, and the soldier looked at Carter, startled. Carter grabbed the man and pulled him through, burying the stiletto to its haft between his ribs on his left side, then slashing left and right.

The soldier never uttered a sound as he collapsed, blood gushing from his side.

Haikkinen pulled him aside and stuffed his body behind one of the equipment consoles as Carter again opened the door. On the other side was a wide balcony than overlooked a vast, equipment-filled cavern. Dozens of technicians were seated at electronic consoles, talking on microphones, adjusting controls, taking measurements from radar screens, or marking tracks on a number of transparent plotting boards. It was very reminiscent of the NASA control center at Houston.

He eased back and closed the door.

"No way in?" Jakes asked.

Carter shook his head. "It's a balcony that overlooks a big control center." He motioned for Haikkinen to take a look.

"What do you want to do?" Jakes asked.

"We'd never get down there undetected," Carter said.

Haikkinen closed the door. He looked rattled. "That's a major operation down there. This has to be one of their bigger bases outside their own country."

Carter looked at his watch again. They were coming up on fifteen minutes. "Can you rig the satchel to blow in fifteen or twenty seconds?"

Haikkinen shook his head. "Wouldn't give us much time to place it and then get away . . ." he began, but then he stopped, understanding dawning in his eyes.

"What?" Jakes asked.

"The charges on the sub are set to go off in less than fifteen minutes," Carter explained. "We'll set this satchel for fifteen seconds, open the door, lob it in the middle of the room, and then get the hell out of here.

By the time they get it all sorted out and try to get the sub out of here, those charges will blow."

"It's your ball game, sir. But it sounds good to me," Jakes said.

Haikkinen was crouched on the floor next to the open satchel adjusting something inside.

It only took him a second or two, and when he was finished he closed the satchel and stood up. A single bare wire stuck out from the flap on each side.

"Connect the wires and we have twenty seconds," Haikkinen said.

Carter sheathed his stiletto, stuffed the gas bomb into his waistband, then pulled out his Luger.

He looked at his watch. Thirteen and a half minutes to go. He took the satchel from Haikkinen.

"You get the door," he said to Jakes.

Jakes nodded and stepped to the door.

Carter turned to Haikkinen. "Ready?"

The young man nodded.

"Do it," Carter said.

Haikkinen quickly connected the wires. Jakes started to open the door when someone burst into the room from the outer balcony.

Carter spun around, bringing up his Luger, as two crewmen from the Chinese sub came in. He fired twice, hitting them both. Then he spun back.

"Now!" he shouted.

Jakes yanked open the door, and Carter stepped onto the balcony, heads below turning up to him. Someone was shouting something. And a siren began to wail as he swung the heavy satchel over his head and let it go, the bag arcing high out over the room.

He turned and raced back to the operations room. Jakes and Haikkinen were at the outer door, firing down toward the sub.

Carter pulled out his gas bomb, thumbed the trigger,

and tossed it over Jakes's shoulder, out the open door,
and down onto the dock.

The gas was effective immediately.

Haikkinen fired another shot, and all three of them
scrambled out the door, along the balcony, and down
the stairs.

Halfway down, a tremendous explosion shook the
entire hillside, partially collapsing the balcony above
them, sending shards of glass blowing straight out
across the water, and bringing rocks and dirt down
from the ceiling.

Crewmen were scrambling out of the submarine as
Haikkinen and Jakes hit the dock, and they opened fire.

Haikkinen went down, the back of his head blown
off, and Jakes was slammed to the left over a pile of
boulders.

Carter, still on the stairs, dropped to a half crouch
and fired four shots in quick succession, hitting at least
three of the crewmen. The others ducked back into the
boat.

Carter leaped down the last couple of stairs, grabbed
Jakes's arm, and pulled him to his feet.

"Arte!" Jakes shouted.

"He's dead," Carter said, racing as fast as he could
with Jakes down the dock and up onto the catwalk.

Several more shots were fired at them from the sub,
but Carter kept going.

The catwalk ended at a thick metal door in the rock
wall above the water. Just as they reached the door, it
opened.

Carter raised his Luger and fired point-blank into the
face of the guard who had been standing outside when
they had swum in.

The guard was thrown backward by the force of the
9mm slug hitting his cheek just below his left eye.

His legs were still twitching as Carter dragged Jakes

over his body and along the catwalk.

Halfway along the catwalk, the wind and blowing water funneling into the cavern, a shot ricocheted off the walkway. A moment later, as Carter turned back with his own gun, two shots thudded into Jakes's body.

Carter fired three shots in quick succession, and then the firing pin snapped on an empty chamber.

He raced the rest of the way down the catwalk and around the corner beneath the overhang, where he laid Jakes down. He pulled out another clip and reloaded the Luger, then bent down to check on Jakes.

The man was dead. He had taken two rounds in his back. One had evidently penetrated a lung, the other had pierced his heart.

Carter looked at his watch. He had nine minutes before the other two charges attached to the sub went off.

Someone was on the path above!

Carter ducked around the overhang in time to see a half-dozen Chinese men hurrying down the path.

He stepped out into the open and fired four shots in rapid succession up the path.

At least three of the soldiers went down.

Carter ducked back. They would pin him down here until it was too late.

''Sorry, Paul,'' Carter said, looking down at Jakes's body. He pushed the dead seaman over the edge, then shoved his Luger into his waistband and jumped into the channel.

The waves were very strong, but he was just at the edge of the tidal race into the cavern, so he was able to swim out past the rocks and around toward the west.

Behind him, above on the path, the remaining soldiers scrambled the rest of the way past the overhang and headed back into the cavern.

The surf was very bad. In the troughs Carter could manage a couple of strokes, but then the breaker would bury him, tumbling him end over end toward the shore.

He was just coming ashore beyond the rocks when a tremendous explosion lifted the front of the rock cliffs away from the hill.

A split second later, a second, much larger explosion lit up the sky, blowing out more of the cliff face.

Carter staggered ashore on the beach, rocks and smoke and flames still shooting out of the vast opening in the hillside to the east.

It had been felt all over the island, and probably had been seen and heard on Hiva Faui. Everyone would know what had happened here.

Carter tore off the wet suit top as he hurried away from the surf pounding the beach, then headed west the last mile or so to where the *Starfish* was scheduled to pick them up.

It was no longer raining, but the wind was strong, and the sky was still overcast. He had no trouble finding the rendezvous spot. It was near where he had found the outrigger canoe the previous night.

Carter was standing on the beach looking out to sea when he saw a flash of light well offshore to the west.

It was most likely the *Starfish*. But she was much too far to the west. . . .

Seconds later he saw another flash, this time even farther west and definitely farther out to sea.

Captain Petti had warned them that if the Chinese sub came back, he would have to stand off.

Carter watched for another five minutes, but there was nothing. Once again he was stranded on Natu Faui.

THIRTEEN

Nick Carter turned away from the ocean and looked up the beach in both directions. The outrigger canoes that had been tied up just off the beach were gone now. It was very possible, he thought, that the natives had gone on another raid of the satellite receiving station. Either that or they had hidden their boats after the one had turned up missing last night.

It was very early in the afternoon, but Carter felt a sense of detachment. He had not had much rest in the past forty-eight hours. But he could not quit now.

The base here on Natu Faui was destroyed. The *Starfish* would probably play cat and mouse with the sub for a day or so, and then the Chinese boat would be ordered back home.

Which left only Governor Albert Rondine and his setup on these islands.

The man was probably working for the Chinese. At least Carter figured he was. But what was his motivation? Simple greed?

Whatever it was, the man held the power of life and death over these people. He was also the apparent master of the Chinese peasants living on Hiva Faui.

Finally there was Gabrielle. Carter could not get her

154

out of his mind. What they had had together, however brief it was, had been wonderful. He wanted to hear from her own lips that everything she had told him was a lie.

He headed up the beach toward the west, his stride long and steady. There was a possibility, he figured, however slight, that the *Starfish* had left even before the shore party had gotten aboard. It would mean the patrol would probably be in the vicinity of the beach down from the volcano. The area was several miles to the west. He wanted to see if they were still there. If not, he would find another outrigger and make the trip back to Hiva Faui one more time.

For a time, as he walked, he thought about all the strange things that had happened so far on this assignment. Most of all of his misjudgments. Fenster, whom he was certain was somehow involved in all of this, apparently was innocent. Gabrielle he had misjudged from the beginning. He wondered if he was misjudging her situation still.

The beach curved in toward the south, the jungle coming right down to the water. He had to wade through the gentle waves, the water protected here by the outcropping of land, to get to the other side.

Across the lagoon a small boat was washed up on the beach. There were several figures lying in the sand beside it.

Carter remained where he was for several long seconds, scanning the line of the beach and the jungle to the far point of land.

There was no movement. Nothing lived across the lagoon.

He splashed through the hip-deep water around the last of the vegetation, and then he was running down the beach, his Luger in hand.

As he got closer he could see that there definitely had been a fight between the shore patrol and the natives.

The boat on the beach was one of the sixteen-man inflatables. It had been punctured several times by arrows and was partially deflated.

He reached the first of the bodies. He turned it over. It was one of the young crewmen. He had not died of arrow wounds, however. He had been shot with a rifle at least four times. Twice in the chest, once in the throat, and once just below his nose, destroying most of his upper lip.

There were four of them. All had died of gunshot wounds. Carter straightened up and looked inland.

The shore party had come here, had been attacked by the natives, but had nevertheless managed to get off the beach.

Four of them had survived to make it back to the boat. Here they had been cut down by the Chinese patrol. It meant there were still Communist soldiers on the island.

Each of the crewmen carried an M-16 automatic rifle with a stainless steel wire stock and plastic grips.

Carter took one of the weapons, then gathered the ammunition from all four bodies, coming up with a total of five clips of forty rounds each.

He pulled the arrows out of the inflatable and found the pump and repair kit in one of the compartments. The fuel tank and the large outboard motor did not seem to be damaged.

Within a half hour he had repaired the half-dozen punctures and had inflated the three compartments that had been damaged.

The boat was seaworthy again. It would get him back to Hiva Faui a lot faster than an outrigger.

In some of the other compartments were supplies of canned water, some rations, and other equipment. There was even a pair of aluminum paddles with extension handles in case the motor did not work. He could get back to Hiva Faui no matter what.

Slowly he manhandled the heavy raft around so that it was facing outward toward the sea. Then he stopped, straightened up, and looked back toward the volcano rising up into the overcast sky.

The shore party had landed here, and the men had pushed their way inland. Their orders: destroy the dish antenna and projection equipment at the native meeting place Carter had described.

Four of them were dead here on the beach. How about the others? Where were they? Were all of them dead?

Captain Petti said he would be sending an officer, a chief petty officer, and twelve crewmen. It was all he could spare. There were four crewmen here. That left the officer, the petty officer, and eight crewmen.

No way, Carter thought, I can't leave without finding out what happened to them.

He shoved the extra ammunition clips into his waistband and headed up the beach onto the trail presumably blazed by the *Starfish* patrol.

A hundred yards inland the petty officer lay on his side with an arrow through his neck, a huge amount of blood beside him. His nametag said *Jones*.

A half mile farther, two more of the crewmen lay dead, their bodies penetrated by arrows. Here it looked as if the patrol had been attacked and had made a stand, apparently driving off their attackers. Ahead and on either side of the trail were at least two dozen bodies of natives.

It was such a terrible waste, Carter thought. The natives were not really at fault. They had been incited to this by the Chinese.

Carter pushed farther inland, moving higher on the slopes of the foothills at the base of the volcano. Away from the sea, the wind blew only in the treetops. Here at the floor of the jungle it was nearly still, and it was becoming hot.

He stopped and peeled off the wet suit bottoms, tossing them aside. His stiletto was bare on his forearm, and his Luger was stuffed into the waistband of his shorts. He carried the spare ammunition clips in his left hand and the M-16 in his right. He was becoming angry. The farther inland he went, the more bodies he saw, and the angrier he got.

He came across three more of the *Starfish*'s crew who had been cut down by arrows. Only their bodies had been mutilated afterward. All had been disemboweled, and their genitals had been cut off.

Carter shivered despite the increasing heat and humidity. The officer and three crewmen were all that was left of the shore party. All that were still unaccounted for. But Carter feared if he continued inland, he might be forced to engage some natives, which he did not want to do.

He turned around to start back to the inflatable. And stopped suddenly. He held his breath and listened. In the vague distance he thought he heard something, but it was just the sound of the waves pounding on the beaches and rocks. There was nothing else. The jungle was silent. As if it were waiting for something.

The Chinese troops would probably not be on this side of the island now. When they heard the explosion they had probably all hurried back to their base to find out what happened.

Still, there were four men unaccounted for. Carter decided he had to find out what had happened to them.

Carter checked to make sure the M-16 was ready to fire, then he stepped around the gruesome remains of the three crewmen and headed up the track through the jungle.

The land rose up sharply from this point, and the *Starfish* patrol had gone up into the hills toward the dish antenna. He and Gabrielle had come to the amphitheater and the dish antenna from the opposite direction, but here the land was essentially the same, the jungle valley to the east and the hills rising to the volcano to the west.

Carter climbed, stopping now and then to scan the valley below, but there was no movement, and everything was quiet.

At the crest of the hill he headed south, almost missing the spot where the dish antenna had been located. He remembered it because of the lightning-struck tree. The tree was still there, but the dish antenna was gone. There were no signs of a fight here. It was very possible that the Chinese, knowing that a patrol was coming—possibly warned by Governor Rondine—had come up here and removed the antenna. They had probably done this before when other U.S. Navy patrols had come ashore.

Carter got down on his hands and knees by the tree and began digging around in the dirt with his stiletto. Almost at once he came up with the end of a cable with a connector. The cable ran directly down the hill in the direction of the amphitheater. The Chinese had unplugged their antenna and had moved it. Probably to a hiding place not far from there.

Carter looked up the hill toward the volcano. Probably up there somewhere. No one would go there looking for it. And even if he did, there would be millions of places to hide the antenna in the natural cracks and crevices in the volcanic rock.

He sheathed his stiletto, grabbed the M-16 where he had leaned it up against the tree, and headed down the hill, the rocks hard on his bare feet.

From here the patrol would have gone directly down the hill to the amphitheater to dismantle the projection equipment. Afterward the survivors had gone back to the beach, where they had been gunned down by the Chinese. Their officer and two of the crewmen had been killed between here and there.

Near the bottom of the hill Carter slowed down, coming at length to the spot where he had pulled up the projection cable and had cut out a fifteen-foot section.

He crept the rest of the way to the edge of the cliff that led down into the meeting place and looked over.

The place had been the scene of a bloodbath. There were at least twenty bodies scattered around the amphitheater. Most of them were bare-chested natives. But among them he saw at least one body clad in dungarees.

There was no movement below. Only the wind in the treetops made any sound.

He crawled back away from the edge, then stood up and made his way around the rim of the natural depression, coming at the bottom to the path that led back into the bowl.

The officer who had led the patrol lay dead on the path, hacked to pieces by what must have been at least a half-dozen machete-wielding natives. His body was horribly mutilated. His left arm was severed from his torso, his spine was nearly chopped out of his body, and the entire back of his head had been peeled back, revealing his brain.

One of the crewmen lay beneath a pile of four natives just within the amphitheater, and the third crewman lay in the middle of the meeting area.

Blood and mangled bodies were everywhere.

Carter started to turn away when a small noise, like a wounded animal or a crying baby, startled him, and he spun around, bringing up the M-16 and flicking off the safety.

It was silent in the amphitheater for a long second. The noise had come from up front, near the altar. There was a pile of bodies on and around the stone.

Carter started forward when the whimpering came

again. It was definitely human, and it came from near the altar. Someone was still alive.

He hurried forward to the altar, picking his way around the bodies. He leaned the rifle against the stone and gently pulled one of the bodies from the pile.

Bob Tieggs, his face covered with blood, looked up at him.

"Christ," Carter breathed.

"Oh . . . Carter . . ." Tieggs croaked.

Carter pulled the other bodies from the wounded pilot. He had been cut deeply on the shoulder, probably with a machete, and an arrow stuck out from his left thigh. He had lost a lot of blood.

"Hang on," Carter said. He jumped up and hurried back to the body of the crewman just in from the path. He had been carrying a small musette bag with a red cross on it.

He grabbed the first aid kit and the canteen on the crewman's hip, and went back to Tieggs. He helped him drink, which seemed to revive him somewhat.

"Am I glad to see you, Carter," Tieggs said, his voice weak.

"What the hell are you doing here, Bob?" Carter asked. He opened the first aid kit and found the bandages and disinfectant.

"I went up to the governor's place like you asked me to do . . . to see if I could find out what happened to Gabrielle . . . to his wife. They were busy as hell up there. I watched from up in the hills."

Carter took out his stiletto. "The arrow has to come out, Bob."

Tieggs swallowed hard, but he nodded. "I watched as they started taking off in their helicopters. I saw the governor and his wife leaving. I figured they were coming out here to watch the show."

"How'd you get here?" Carter asked. He pulled out

a syringe of morphine and some cotton. He swabbed an area of Tieggs's hip with the disinfectant.

"I got into their compound and managed to steal one of the helicopters. When I got here I saw all the fighting, so I landed on the beach and came up."

"No sign of the governor?"

"None," Tieggs said.

Carter gave him the shot of morphine.

"I was lucky. I got up here, and it was mostly all over," Tieggs said, but then his voice began to slur, and after a moment he blinked and grinned. "God Almighty, she's beautiful . . ." he mumbled.

Carter poured some of the disinfectant over the blade of his stiletto, and then over and around the arrow wound.

Tieggs did not flinch. He kept grinning and mumbling as Carter carefully cut deeply around the arrow. Within a few seconds he had cut the arrowhead out of Tieggs's thigh, the blood welling up slowly.

He poured some more disinfectant into the wound and bandaged it firmly. He did the same for the wound on Tieggs's shoulder.

It had taken less than ten minutes. Tieggs was sweating profusely.

"Don't feel so good, old man . . ." he slurred. It was the loss of blood and the effects of the morphine.

Carter bundled up the first aid things back in the bag, threw it and the M-16 over his shoulder, and carefully picked up Tieggs. On the path, Carter turned south around the volcano toward the beach. It was several miles away, and Tieggs was heavy. The spunky helicopter pilot had passed out, but he came to when they stopped by the spring and Carter splashed some cool water on his face.

He winced when he tried to move, and his eyes fluttered. "Christ," he swore out loud, his voice ragged but a lot stronger.

He had passed out less than an hour ago, but already his color was a lot better.

"How do you feel?" Carter asked.

"Feel? Like a goddamned Mack truck ran over me." He pushed himself up with his good arm. Carter helped him, then gave him the canteen. Tieggs drank the cool spring water, letting a lot of it spill down his chest.

When he was finished he looked from his leg up to Carter. "You do pretty good work for a cop."

"I only did it because I needed another favor."

"It figures," Tieggs said. He glanced toward the trail. "What about the shore party from the sub? Did any of them make it?"

Carter shook his head. "I found four of them on the other side of the island. They were dead. The Chinese killed them."

Tieggs looked back. "There was an explosion. Everyone bugged out. It's the last I remember. Was it you?"

"The Chinese base here is destroyed."

"Where's our sub?"

"Out there someplace, chasing down one of theirs."

"It was based here, on this island, all this time?"

"Yes."

Tieggs whistled. "And you think Governor Rondine is involved somehow."

"He's involved up to his ears. Our sub will take care of theirs, but we have to get to Rondine."

Tieggs grinned, although he was obviously in a great deal of pain. "And you'd prefer that I fly the chopper."

"Are you up to it? You know your way around those things a hell of a lot better than I do."

Tieggs shrugged with his good shoulder as best he could. "Who the hell knows until we try it."

Carter refilled the canteen, then hefted the first aid kit and the M-16, and picked up Tieggs, who protested.

"I want you to save your strength for flying. I'll do the walking for the both of us."

They passed the spot where Fenster's helicopter had been shot down. As far as Carter knew there were no missile emplacements on the island. His helicopter had probably been brought down by a bazooka or some other hand-held weapon carried by one of the Chinese patrols.

Gradually the land began to drop away from the volcano's southeast side, and the jungle became much thicker and almost impossible to break through until they came across the trail he and Gabrielle had walked up.

A half hour later they could hear the surf. Ten minutes after that they came to the beach. The helicopter Tieggs had taken from Governor Rondine's compound was parked several hundred yards farther west on the beach. But there were men standing around it.

Carter had just stepped out of the jungle, when he spotted the helicopter and then the men. He ducked back into the undergrowth and laid Tieggs down.

"Chinese?" Tieggs asked.

"I think so," Carter said. He gave Tieggs his Luger. "There're only a couple of rounds left. But it's better than nothing. I'll be back."

"Don't get yourself killed," Tieggs said, but Carter had already gone back into the jungle.

He worked his way parallel to the beach, taking great care to make absolutely no noise, although the crash of the surf coming up on the beach was loud enough to drown out practically any sound.

It took Carter nearly fifteen minutes to work his way through the thick undergrowth to a spot opposite the helicopter. It did not look as if the machine had been damaged. There were five Chinese Communist soldiers dressed in World War II Japanese Army uniforms. One of them sat with his back against the landing gear, one stood by the water's edge on the far side of the machine, and the other three stood together on the side closest to Carter.

Carter made sure the safety was off and that a round was in the M-16's firing chamber. He flipped the selector switch to single shot, then settled down on his right heel, his left elbow supported by his left knee, the weapon's sling wrapped around his shoulder and wrist.

There could be no mistakes, he told himself as he brought the soldier by the water's edge into his sights. He brought the barrel down and to the right, quickly lining up with the man leaning against the landing gear. Then he flipped the selector switch to full automatic as he brought the weapon up and around to take in the three men standing.

The first two shots would come dangerously close to the helicopter. Depending upon which way the nearest three jumped, they would either be clear of the machine, or they would be right in line with it.

There was no other option. It was either this way or he would lose Governor Rondine and Gabrielle.

He pushed the selector switch back to single fire and once again lined up with the man at the water's edge.

He had just started to squeeze, when the soldier spun around, bringing up his rifle.

Something was happening down the beach in the direction Carter had left Tieggs.

One of the soldiers nearest Carter shouted something, and the soldier leaning against the chopper's landing gear started to get up.

Carter squeezed off one shot that hit the soldier by the beach in the spine, doubling him over before he went down.

He aimed at the soldier by the landing gear, fired one shot that hit him in the leg and brought him down, then he fired two more shots, one hitting the man in the shoulder, the other taking off the right side of his head.

It all happened in barely a few seconds, and Carter flipped the selector switch over to full automatic as he brought the weapon around.

The other three soldiers had turned in the direction of the shots, and Carter opened fire, sweeping right across them, the M-16's slugs ripping a bloody dotted line across their chests.

FOURTEEN

"I figured you might need a little diversionary tactic," Tieggs said as Carter helped him strap into the left-hand seat of the helicopter.

Carter looked at him. Tieggs was a good man. Among the best Carter had run into in his career. "They had rifles. You had a handgun."

"They would never have hit me. The Chinese are all bad shots anyway."

Carter shook his head. "Dumb bastard," he said, laughing. He slammed the door and hurried around to the right side. He climbed up and strapped in as Tieggs painfully flipped the master switch, cracked the throttle, and hit the starter.

The engine turned over, caught, and the rotors began swinging. Slowly at first, but gathering speed. Tieggs took the controls in his left hand, his feet on the pedals, and he glanced at Carter.

"Is your life insurance up-to-date? Here goes nothing," Tieggs said, and they lifted raggedly off the sand, the wind carrying them dangerously close to the treetops along the beach before he got them straightened out with a cry of pain.

Carter gritted his teeth but said nothing. Tieggs was a *damned* good man.

They swung out over the water, then headed north directly toward Hiva Faui, Tieggs cranking the power full.

"Let's set down at the receiver station," Carter said.

Tieggs glanced at him. Sweat was pouring from his brow. He nodded.

"We'll have the medics give you something to keep you going. I'll need my clothes and some more ammunition."

They hit an air pocket, and Tieggs nearly lost it but recovered nicely. He grinned weakly. "What I think I need is a couple of pints of O positive. Might make a difference."

Carter was about to ask Tieggs if he wanted him to take over the controls when the pilot stiffened and nodded toward the north. Carter looked out the Plexiglas.

There were at least a hundred outriggers of various sizes, each filled with natives, heading north through the large waves.

Tieggs swooped a little lower so that they came right over the center of the flotilla. The men in the boats looked up. Some of them shook their fists, others waved their machetes menacingly skyward. A few even shot arrows up at them.

Then they passed them and were climbing again.

"They're on their way to attack the base!" Tieggs said.

"Let's go back," Carter said, looking out over the water.

"What?"

"Let's go back over them. Low. Right on top of them. Let's see if we can discourage a few of them."

"Have you seen the size of the waves they're paddling through, for Christ's sake?"

"I've seen them," Carter said. He opened the door, and the wind took it back with a bang. The cabin was filled with wind.

Tieggs swooped around and slowed down to cut some of the wind in the cabin. Carter had pulled out the M-16.

"Get right down on top of them," Carter said. "If we can stop the attack here and now, we just might save a lot of lives . . . our people as well as theirs."

They came down barely above wave height and hovered, the open door on Carter's side facing toward the oncoming canoes.

Carter took careful aim at the lead canoe and squeezed off a short burst that kicked up water over the bow.

Tieggs pulled back up, then came down again just ahead of the canoes, and Carter fired off a few more short bursts.

The natives were all shouting and screaming now. Some of them were shooting arrows, and a couple even threw spears. But they had stopped moving and were simply riding up and down with the waves, some of the paddlers merely holding their bows into the wind.

"They'll wait until we're gone and then continue," Tieggs shouted. "Unless you kill them all."

Carter looked back at him. Tieggs was right. He nodded. "Let's get back to the receiver station. At least we can warn them." He managed to pull the door closed while they were stationary, and then Tieggs brought them around and back up to cruising altitude.

Before they had gone very far, Carter looked back over his shoulder at the outriggers. The natives were once again bent to the task of getting to Hiva Faui.

Even without the constant goading that the Chinese projection system gave to the natives, they would continue to attack the receiver station for a long time to come unless someone was brought in to work with them. It would have to be done very soon. Possibly even using the same visual propaganda techniques that the Chinese used to incite them to their attacks in the first place.

Smoke rose high into the sky in ragged plumes from the far end of Hiva Faui. It was somewhere in or around the town, Carter guessed. It was anyone's guess what was happening there with the Chinese now that the base had been destroyed and the governor apparently fled.

There were armed technicians at the main gate and at various spots around the perimeter fence of the receiver station, and when the helicopter set down on the grass in front of the administration building, the station manager, Justin Owen, came running.

Before the rotors had completely stopped, Carter jumped out and hurried around to Tieggs's side.

Owen had reached them. "What the hell happened over there?" he shouted.

"Get a medic. Bob has been hurt," Carter said, popping the door open.

Other people were coming up to the helicopter, and Owen called for one of them to get the doctor. Then he helped Carter lift Tieggs out of the machine. They laid him on the grass. He was in a lot of pain again, and the wound at his leg was leaking through the bandages.

"Is there anyone else on this base who can fly a helicopter?" Carter asked.

Owen shook his head. "We've called for our support aircraft, but it'll be a day or so before it gets here. They're going crazy in the city. Ever since the big explosion on Natu Faui."

"The natives are on their way here right now," Carter said. "They're a couple of hours out. Maybe a little farther, but they'll be here."

"Damn," Owen swore.

The base doctor came from the administration building at a dead run. Two technicians carrying a stretcher were right behind him.

Carter turned back to Tieggs. "They'll fix you up, Bob. As soon as possible, I want you to refuel the chopper and get it over to the governor's mansion."

"I'll get there," Tieggs said thickly.

"He's going nowhere," the doctor said, taking Tieggs's wrist.

"He'll have to, Doctor," Carter said, getting up. "Unless you can come up with another helicopter pilot."

"And if it kills him?" the doctor snapped, looking up.

Carter shook his head. "No," he said. "Just do the best you can. It's important."

"What's going on?" Owen said. "Can you tell me that much?"

"No time now," Carter said. "But I'll need a jeep." He headed across to the administration building where his bags were.

"It'll be out front in five minutes," Owen called after him.

Upstairs, Carter peeled off his shorts and climbed into a cool shower, letting the water cascade down his body, the spray sharp and wonderful.

With or without Tieggs and the helicopter, Carter figured he had probably lost the governor. The man could be hundreds of miles away by now. Very possibly on his way to China or to any of a thousand places where he would be safe.

It was just possible, however, that there would be some indication left behind at the mansion telling where they had gone. Or there might even be someone left behind—staff or one of his goons—who might be persuaded to tell where the governor had gone.

He stepped out of the shower just as a technician came into his room with a cold beer and a sandwich.

"Mr. Owen thought you might be hungry, sir," the man said.

"Thanks," Carter said, and the technician left.

Carter quickly got dressed, then rapidly took apart his Luger, oiled the parts, and reassembled it. He loaded the clip and put another in his pocket. He wiped Hugo's blade with oil and strapped another gas bomb to his thigh.

He grabbed the sandwich and beer on the way out the door.

Downstairs he stopped at Owen's office. The station manager was busy giving orders for the defense of the station. This would be the first native attack the technicians would be ready for.

"I'm going into town to find the governor," Carter said.

Owen looked up from the phone. "Can you tell me what happened over on Natu Faui? We heard the explosion."

"There was a Communist Chinese base over there. We destroyed it."

Owen looked at Carter, dumbfounded. But then he slowly nodded his head. "And the governor? He's working for the Chinese?"

"Something like that."

Again Owen nodded. "I'll send Bob along with the helicopter if and when the doc clears him."

"Appreciate it," Carter said, and he turned and hurried outside, tossing the half-full beer bottle into a trash can.

A jeep with keys in it was parked just outside. Carter jumped in and headed down to the main gate. Before he came to a complete halt, the technicians opened the gate for him. He waved and sped up, then he was down the hill and around the curve.

He drove as fast as he could, mindful of the fact that the Chinese had booby-trapped this road with downed trees on blind curves more than once in the past forty-eight hours.

But the drive into town was uneventful. The day was warm. The sky was beginning to clear in the east, and the wind had begun to calm down, although there were still large waves roaring onto the beach.

The hotel and Madame Leone's, next door, were on fire, smoke rising high into the afternoon sky. At least a hundred Orientals were gathered in the square in front of the burning buildings. As Carter came around the last curve into town, the crowd was shouting something, but he couldn't quite make it out. They spotted him almost immediately and came running to try to intercept him as he came around the lower road.

Carter sped up, pulled out his Luger, and fired a couple of shots over their heads.

The crowd fell back, and he was around the corner, past the square, and was soon screaming up the hill, expertly negotiating the switchback road. There did not seem to be anyone around, but there was a lot of debris littering the roadway. It was as if they had had a riot up here.

At the top he had to swerve to avoid a large wooden crate, but then he was around the last switchback and heading along the crest of the hill to the governor's compound.

The main gate was closed, but it was unmanned as far as Carter could see. Without reducing speed he ducked down as he hit the gate, slamming one side off its hinges, the jeep slewing first left, then right before he got it under control again.

There was a large Mercedes sedan and two small

trucks parked just down from the house, but the helicopters were gone.

Nothing looked disturbed, nor did the house look abandoned. The French flag flew from the pole just down from the driveway at the front of the house.

Carter pulled up and jumped out of the car as a young Oriental woman came out onto the veranda. Carter took the stairs two at a time up to her.

"Governor Rondine is not here this afternoon, sir," she said.

"Where did he go?" Carter asked.

"I do not know, sir," the woman replied.

"I'll just wait in his study, then," Carter said, brushing past her and hurrying across the veranda. At the French doors he hesitated a moment as he watched the young woman's reflection in the glass. She pulled out a long knife from beneath her smock and silently charged.

At the last moment, Carter stepped aside, grabbed her wrist, and quickly twisted her arm. She dropped the knife with a little cry and stepped back as he let go.

He picked up the knife and tossed it over the railing. "Where did the governor and his wife go?" he demanded.

The woman was rubbing her wrist. She shook her head as she backed up. Suddenly she spun around and hurried across the veranda and down the stairs.

Carter pulled out Wilhelmina and entered the house. Two young Chinese boys stood in the entryway to the left. When they saw Carter they bolted up the stairs. A clock chimed somewhere, and he could hear music coming from upstairs.

He went through the living room and the dining room to the back of the house. To the left was the music room, beyond which was a small sitting room and then the kitchen. To the right was the hall that led to the back veranda. A set of double doors were closed.

He tried them. They were locked. He stepped back, brought up his Luger, and fired two shots into the lock, then kicked the doors open.

A Chinese man in a khaki uniform was seated at a radio set. He jumped up and spun around, a submachine gun in his hands.

Carter fired two shots, the first hitting the man in the chest, the second in his throat, blood splattering everywhere as he was thrown backward against the radio, his weapon clattering to the floor.

Carter kicked the gun aside, made sure the man was dead, then looked at the radio. Someone was calling. Deep in the static. It sounded like French, but Carter could not be sure.

A helicopter came in low over the house, then swung around to the east.

Carter went to the window and looked outside. He could hear the machine on the other side of the house. It sounded as if it was coming down for a landing.

He turned around. There were three Oriental men in khaki uniforms just outside the doorway. They each held a submachine gun pointed at Carter.

"You will please to put your weapon on the desk," one of them said, his English very bad.

Carter hesitated.

"Please. We do not want to kill you just yet, Mr. Carter."

Carter walked over to the desk and laid down his Luger, then he stepped away a few paces.

"That is very wise, Mr. Carter. Now, who is coming here in the helicopter? Is it your colleague from the spy satellite base?"

"He's a helicopter pilot, nothing more," Carter said. "Where is Governor Rondine?"

The man grinned. "Your submarine is a very long

way from here now, Mr. Carter. You have done much damage to us, and now we will find out all about you and who you work for.''

The temperature in the room seemed to drop by twenty degrees. Nevertheless Carter smiled.

''Yes,'' he said. ''One of your submarines has been destroyed, your base ruined, and very soon your second submarine will be rendered useless as well. I don't suppose you'll get a promotion for this.''

There was a commotion out in the corridor. It sounded to Carter like someone swearing in French. He glanced at his Luger on the desk, but the man who had been doing the talking raised his weapon a little higher.

''You will die if you try it.''

One of the soldiers was shoved aside, and a large, burly man barreled his way into the room. He looked at Carter.

''That's him,'' he said in French.

''What are you doing here?'' the Chinese man asked in French.

''I've got my orders. The governor wants him,'' the big man said. He turned back to Carter. He carried a large Beretta automatic. ''You will come with me voluntarily, or I shall kneecap you, Monsieur Carter. Do you understand?'' he asked in English.

Carter nodded. It had been he who had arrived in the helicopter, not Tieggs. Carter shrugged. ''I don't have much of a choice.''

''No,'' the Frenchman said. He stepped away from the doorway and motioned Carter outside.

They went back through the dining room and living room, out onto the veranda, and down to the driveway. A large French military helicopter was parked just beyond the flagpole. Two men waited by it.

The three Chinese men had come out of the house,

but they remained up on the veranda. Carter looked back at them. There was some kind of a power struggle going on here. But at the moment he could not see how he could turn it to his advantage. The Frenchman he was with was definitely a pro.

They marched across the driveway to the helicopter, and Carter was directed to climb into the rear compartment, where he was manacled to one of the seat supports after he had strapped in.

The Frenchman who had brought him down from the house went back up to the veranda to speak with the Chinese soldiers. The other two Frenchmen climbed into the helicopter, one of them at the controls, and he started the engine.

A minute later the other one came back, climbed in, and without a word they lifted off.

Almost immediately the pilot stiffened. "We have company," he said in French. "Looks like a small helicopter."

They swung around and headed toward town as Tieggs, in the smaller helicopter, swung past them from the left.

Carter's captor turned back to him. "Who is in the machine?"

"It's no one. Just a pilot from the base."

The man turned back. "Shoot him down," he said calmly.

"No!" Carter shouted, sitting forward.

They swung around, the pilot expertly bringing them up behind Tieggs.

"You bastards!" Carter shouted. "He's done nothing to you!"

The Frenchman turned back with his Beretta and jammed the barrel into Carter's face. "I will blow your head off, *monsieur*, if you are not quiet."

The French pilot was doing something with what

looked like a weapons tracking and locking system. Out ahead, Tieggs apparently understood he was in trouble, because he was taking evasive actions.

"Now," the pilot said. He punched a button. A rocket streaked from their underbelly and in less than three seconds closed on Tieggs's machine. There was a brief pause, then the explosion.

FIFTEEN

Nick Carter kept seeing the explosion that destroyed Tieggs's helicopter. Tieggs never had a chance, although he had known what was about to happen.

Afterward they had swung out over the water to the southwest but had kept low, presumably to keep well under any radar or detection systems even though there was nothing out here but undeveloped islands.

Carter sat back. Right now there wasn't a damned thing he could do, he thought. The governor was working for the Chinese. Evidently Rondine swung some weight, otherwise the soldiers back at the house would not have deferred so easily to his henchmen. But Carter had wanted to see the man, and he would soon be getting his chance.

The military chopper they were in was very fast. Nevertheless it took them the better part of two hours before they swung around the western side of a large, jungle-choked island, came in low over a lagoon, then slowly followed a wide river or channel several hundred yards up from the beach.

They were almost on top of the yacht before Carter spotted it, and he realized that from more than a few hundred feet in the air it would be virtually invisible

179

despite its size, which Carter estimated to be at least 150 feet.

About a half mile beyond the yacht, they came down in a narrow clearing. As the rotors slowed, the Frenchmen got out of the machine, and the one who had brought Carter out of the house opened the rear door and unlocked his manacles.

He stepped back, his Beretta out, as one of the other men came around and quickly frisked Carter, coming up with his stiletto but not the gas bomb. He gave the blade to the man with the gun.

"As soon as you are done here, come down to the boat. I think he wants to leave at dark."

"*Oui*, Claude," the man said.

Carter's captor motioned with the Beretta, and they started down the path. Behind them the other two men were shoving the helicopter down the slope toward some overhanging trees. When they were finished, Carter suspected there would be little or nothing to be seen from the air.

It was very hot. The weather had cleared, and there wasn't a breath of air.

If they were leaving tonight after dark, they would probably run through the night without lights. By morning they would be far enough away from everything and not arouse the suspicion of anyone. Carter was sure he had seen a Liberian registry flag flying from the mast above the bridge deck.

He pondered his situation. Once he was aboard the boat and at sea, there would not be a lot he could do. Forget a rescue. And there would be little likelihood that he would get off the boat alive.

He stopped and turned around.

"*Allons! Allons!*" the big man shouted.

Carter let his eyes roll back in his head and flutter. "Christ . . ." he whispered, and he fell forward as if in a faint.

The Frenchman instinctively reached out. Carter fumbled with the man's gun hand as if he were seeking support. Too late the big man understood that it was a ruse. Carter drove forward and up, butting the man's chin with his head. At the same moment he twisted the Beretta sharply to the right, breaking the man's wrist with a loud pop.

The man cried out, then swore loudly in French.

Carter stepped back, kneed the man in the groin, then drove a right hook into his jaw that sent him flying backward onto the ground. The man was out cold.

All of that took less than five seconds, and Carter was sure the scuffle had not alerted the helicopter crew. Nevertheless he grabbed the automatic and crouched by the side of the path, waiting for any signs that an alarm had been sounded.

But there was nothing other than the soft, jungle sounds of insects and birds.

Carter retrieved his stiletto from the downed man, and with the manacles that had been used to hold him in the back seat of the helicopter, he manacled the Frenchman to a small tree. He stuffed a handkerchief into the man's mouth and used his belt to hold it in place.

On the path he looked down toward where the yacht was tied, then up in the direction of the helicopter. If he went back to the helicopter to take care of the two crewmen, there was a very good chance he would have to use the Beretta. Someone from the yacht would hear it, and his element of surprise would be lost.

On the other hand, the crewmen would be coming down to the yacht within a very short time. Unless he was finished with what he wanted to do, they would be on top of him.

The latter was the more easily acceptable risk to Carter, and he headed quickly down the path toward the governor's yacht.

Rondine was intelligent. He had apparently expected his little island kingdom to come to an end sooner or later, and he had prepared for it with this yacht as his escape hatch.

In all likelihood he had another place picked out and ready for him, probably with the help of the Chinese.

The yacht was the *Mariposa*, Spanish for butterfly. She lay at anchor in the middle of the narrow channel. A couple of small motor launches were pulled up to the shore.

Carter held back within the protection of the jungle as he looked out at the activity. A couple of crewmen had gone over the side near the stern of the yacht, evidently to check on the propellers or the rudder. Several crewmen were visible on deck, and the ship's radar antenna was slowly spinning.

They were alert and ready for intruders.

Closer, two crewmen waited by the pair of motor launches pulled up to the river bank. Carter, his captor, and the two helicopter crewmen were evidently expected. The boatmen kept looking at their watches and glancing up the path.

His only way aboard would be by one of the motor launches. If he could lure the two crewmen out of sight of the yacht, he might be able to take them out.

He pulled out his gas bomb and started to edge around to the left, when the barrel of an automatic touched his cheek.

"Straighten up very slowly, Monsieur Carter."

Carter did as he was told, very slowly, the gas bomb in his left hand, the Beretta in his right.

There was only one of them . . . one of the crew from the helicopter. Carter figured if the noise could be kept down, he would still have a chance.

At that moment, however, the other crewman came up the path with the big Frenchman whom Carter had knocked out. The man did not appear to be happy.

"Louis! Jean!" he shouted. The two men from the motor launch jumped up and came running.

Carter let himself relax as one of them pulled his gas bomb and the Beretta out of his grasp.

Claude, the big Frenchman with the broken wrist, backhanded Carter, knocking him backward but not off his feet.

"*Salaud*," the man hissed.

Carter was smiling. "Send your pals away, and I'd be glad to break your other wrist," he said in French.

The big man was barely able to control his anger as he shoved Carter around and down the path. "The governor will have a few things to say to you, Monsieur Carter. But afterward you will be mine!"

They boarded the two motor launches, and within a minute or so they were climbing aboard the *Mariposa*, a couple of officers and several crewmen watching from the rails.

Carter was taken immediately aft and then into the main salon.

Governor Rondine, wearing a light gauze shirt and white trousers, a gold chain around his immense neck, lounged in a chaise. Gabrielle was seated next to him. She wore a very brief white bikini that was stunning against her tanned olive skin.

There were a dozen other men and similarly dressed women. They were having a light snack and were drinking champagne.

"Ah, Monsieur Carter. Welcome aboard," Governor Rondine boomed jovially.

One of the helicopter crewmen had gone out on deck. He came back with a nylon-webbed deck chair and placed it in the middle of the salon, in front of the governor and his guests.

"You know, I kept asking myself who you were and what you were," the governor said. He waved his hand. "Oh, we knew that you were an investigator sent from Washington. Like the others. But you . . ." he hesitated. "You were different. You caused us much pain."

The crewman had cut away the webbing from the chair's seat.

"The colonel is most unhappy. I'm told that Peking is not happy. You have created a very large problem for us. One, really, that has no solution."

The governor nodded, and several of the ship's crew crowded into the salon and forcibly shoved Carter into the chair, tied him in place, and then stepped aside.

"But I asked myself," the governor continued, "what was it I needed to help alleviate the situation . . . salve the wound, so to speak."

Gabrielle looked very uncomfortable, but most of the other guests seemed to be enjoying this.

"I told myself that I would need information. Who you are, who you work for, and just how you found out about the operations center on Natu Faui. With such information I would have at least something to offer the colonel."

Again the governor nodded. One of the crewmen flipped out a straight razor and came to Carter's side, where he quickly and efficiently cut off Carter's shirt and then his trousers, pulling the rags away from his body until he was seated completely nude, his rear end and testicles exposed by the bottomless chair.

A couple of the women tittered as the crewman put away his blade and stepped aside.

"He dallied with my wife. Most unfortunate . . . for Monsieur Carter," the governor said, and again he nodded.

The crewman went over to a sideboard where the food had been set up.

"Your island kingdom is gone, and you expect the Communists to give you another. Is that it?" Carter asked.

The governor smiled. "He speaks. There is *some* hope for the poor devil."

Carter could not see what the crewman was doing at the sideboard. But he could feel the sweat running down his chest.

"How far do you expect to get in this toy? Our submarine is still—"

"Is a thousand miles from here. There will be no rescue, Monsieur Carter. You will be tortured until you give us the information we require. And then, mercifully, I will kill you."

The crewman at the sideboard turned around. He was holding the fire ring from a chafing dish. He brought it over and set it beneath Carter, then lit the alcohol flame.

Almost immediately Carter could feel the heat on his anus and testicles. He tried to lift himself up, but he could not move more than an inch or so. He started to scoot the chair to one side, but two of the crewmen grabbed the back of the chair and held him in place.

The heat rose.

"Take it away and I'll tell you what you want to know," Carter said, the pain already beginning.

The governor chuckled. "Yes, I think I will do just that, Monsieur Carter." He turned to Gabrielle. "But first, my dear, would you pour me a glass of champagne?"

The pain was rising sharply. Every muscle in Carter's body was straining.

Gabrielle jumped up and looked wildly from Carter to her husband.

"Albert," she said.

Carter could feel a scream building in his chest and rising up his throat.

Rondine laughed. He held out his champagne glass.

"Albert!" Gabrielle screamed.

A moan escaped Carter's lips.

Gabrielle turned, raced to Carter, and kicked the alcohol burner away, then spun back and grabbed the champagne glass from her husband's hand.

The governor was laughing out loud now. "Touching," he said, choking. "Very touching."

Gabrielle broke the champagne glass on the edge of the coffee table, then leaped forward, plunging the ragged glass edge into Rondine's throat, opening a jagged wound that spurted blood. Someone screamed as she viciously jabbed again, this time using the glass as a saw, severing the artery on the left side of his neck before one of the crewmen pulled her off and shoved her aside.

"*Mon Dieu!*" one of the crewmen cried.

"The doctor!" another one shouted.

Through a haze of pain, Carter watched as Rondine thrashed and kicked, his blood pumping everywhere as he tore at his throat with his hands, a terrible, choking sound coming from his mouth.

The guests had all jumped up and moved toward the doorway to the aft deck. One of the men was vomiting. The women were screaming and crying.

Gabrielle had scooped up a large .357 magnum pistol from where it evidently had been stuffed beneath one of the cushions beside the governor, and she waved it around.

"Everyone out of here!" she screamed.

The governor gave one final gasp, looked up at his wife, then rolled over and lay still in a huge puddle of his own blood.

"Everyone out of here!" she screamed again. "He is dead! It is all over!"

She fired a shot, high. It smacked into the door-frame above the guests' heads.

The women screamed again, and everyone crowded through the door.

"Have the captain make the boat ready!" she cried

after them. "You are leaving here."

She came to Carter's side, the tears welling in her eyes as she untied him.

"Can you walk?" she asked.

Carter's stomach was heaving, and the pain below was unspeakable, but his head was clear, and he managed to stand.

He took the .357 from her. "We'll stay aboard. Radio for help." Talking was an effort.

She shook her head wildly. "There is a bomb," she whispered. "I put a bomb in the engine room. This boat will explode tonight at midnight. Everyone aboard will be killed."

"How . . ." Carter began.

"It was meant for you in the hotel or at the base. The colonel gave it to me."

Carter tried to make his mind work. They would be stranded here on this island. The little motor launches wouldn't get them very far. But then he remembered the helicopter. He had flown one before when absolutely necessary, and there would be a radio aboard so that they could signal for help.

He stumbled across the salon to the door as the ship's diesels came to life. Several crewmen were working to bring both motor launches aboard.

Carter stepped out on deck. "Stand back," he shouted. They looked around.

Someone came out of the bridge above. Carter looked up at him. He had a rifle.

"We'll cause you no trouble," Carter said. "We want to get off here. You can take this boat anywhere you want. It'll be days before we'll be found. It'll give you plenty of time."

For a long second or two no one moved or said a thing. Finally the man on the bridge deck put up his rifle.

"Let them go," he said.

"No!" the big Frenchman with the broken wrist suddenly shouted from the starboard deck.

Carter spun around, bringing up the .357 as the man charged. He fired one shot, catching Claude in the chest and sending him backward, his body flipping over the rail and into the river.

Gabrielle emerged from the salon. She carried a first aid kit, some clothing, and a duffle bag with something heavy in it.

Carefully they made their way across the aft deck, then down the boarding ladder into the second motor launch.

Gabrielle undid the line as Carter started the motor, and they were off. Soon the *Mariposa*'s anchor began to come up.

EPILOGUE

They heard the explosion far to the northwest at around midnight from where they were camped near the helicopter.

Carter's burns were more painful than they were serious. It would be weeks, perhaps months, before he would feel completely normal. But Gabrielle assured him that nothing had been permanently damaged.

They had switched on the emergency locator beacon transmitter in the chopper. Sooner or later a high-flying commercial airliner or a ship passing near these islands would pick up the signal and would come to investigate. But in the meantime there were rations aboard the helicopter, more aboard the launch, and there were a dozen varieties of fruit on the island. In the duffle bag Gabrielle had brought from the ship were a half-dozen bottles of excellent champagne.

Carter had slept for several hours, and when he awoke late in the night, they had eaten and talked.

The French police had come out to the islands a few years ago looking for Gabrielle . . . or so Rondine had convinced her.

She had been hidden, and when the investigator left, Rondine had told her that more than ever before her life belonged to him.

"It was Albert or prison in France," she said.

Carter slept again, the pain subsiding somewhat, although he still did not wear trousers.

He was dreaming about the pain and about another sensation that was a cross between pain and pleasure when he awoke in the morning.

Gabrielle looked up, a smile on her lips. "Does it hurt, Nick?" she asked.

"I haven't decided yet," he said, wondering if it would break the mood for him to ask her to turn off the emergency transmitter in the helicopter. . . .

DON'T MISS THE NEXT NEW NICK CARTER SPY THRILLER

NIGHT OF THE WARHEADS

The Killmaster mentally cursed.

This sorry excuse for a soldier was obviously the bodyguard Madrid had provided Mendez. He looked like a leftover from Franco's era and, as such, probably hated Julio Mendez and everything the man stood for, then and now.

The driver was pushing seventy, and also no help. He was already leaning his head back against the seat, as if he were headed directly for siesta.

The two deputies had reached Mendez's "bodyguard." Hubanyo was talking to Mendez, gesturing toward the small building behind him and shaking his head from side to side.

If it was going down, it would be soon now.

There was a tiny ripping sound as Carter's finger began opening the velcro.

Call it *déjà vu*, or call it the sixth sense of the trained killer, that survival instinct had kept the Killmaster alive through many missions.

Or call it the reality of what was: a slight rocking of the old pickup, the monks shifting from single file to fan out in their movement.

And the thump of a rubber tire-cased footstep on the porch behind him.

The driver.

Carter was no language expert, but he knew a little of the local dialect, and Cubanez had taught him more in their short time together.

The driver had spoken pretty decent Spanish, but it suddenly hit Nick that it wasn't the local dialect or even decent peasant Spanish.

It was Mexican-Spanish.

And then he remembered the *huaraches* . . . Mexican peasant shoes.

If a Mexican wanted comfortable footwear to do a big job, he might very well wear what he was most accustomed to . . .

Carter ripped the velcro all the way and filled his hand with the Luger. At the same time, he lurched to the right, out of the chair, and rolled in the air.

The young driver, a toothy grin spreading his mahogany face, stood in the cantina's doorway. His arms were straight out from his body, his hand holding an already barking .357.

The Magnum's slugs made kindling out of the chair back Carter had just vacated.

Carter's back hit the porch just as Wilhelmina belched. It threw his aim off slightly, but it was still a hit.

The slug thudded into the guy's left hip bone, spinning him around. He hit the wall belly first, staining a good chunk of the faded whitewash with his blood before turning again for a second try at the rolling figure.

Carter squeezed off two rounds: one dead center in the guy's gut, the other a head shot.

The Magnum flew from his hands as if on invisible strings, and he was flattened against the wall. He was faceless and his belly was belching blood.

Carter rolled to his belly on the porch, the Luger in his outstretched hands.

All hell had broken loose around him.

Three gunmen had erupted from the bed of the pickup. They all held barking semi-automatic rifles. Their fire was witheringly directed at Hubanyo and Mendez, but most of it was doing nothing more than making scrap out of the Ford.

Carter took all the rest of the dusty scene in one microsecond look-see.

The eight monks were each on one knee. From beneath their robes they had produced everything from Browning hi-powers to .357s.

Hubanyo had wrestled Mendez three-quarters of the way to the buildings, so they were out of the monks' line of fire.

The two deputies and the bodyguard hadn't been so lucky.

The uniformed man lay next to the Ford, his body cut nearly in half. One of the two deputies had made it back to the speaker's platform, where he now lay throwing a little fire—when he could raise his head— toward the pickup. The other deputy had been hit in the right leg and was under the Ford, partially shielded by the front wheels.

He wouldn't last long.

It had all happened fast, maybe ten seconds. And it was happening faster.

Cubanez had already opened up on the monks,

dropping two of them with fast fire from the Galil. The others were hustling to positions behind the stores and in nearby rocks.

The three in the rear of the pickup had been so intent on trying to nail Mendez that they hadn't noticed that their buddy had failed to waste the *Americano* on the porch.

Carter dived through the door of the cantina and crab-walked across the large room. Near the rear he found a window. When it wouldn't open he kicked it out, frame and all, with his booted foot.

He dived through, head first. Hitting the dust with his shoulder, he rolled and came up on his feet like a cat, the Luger ready to blow hell out of whomever its dark, deadly snout could find.

Through the windshield and the rear window of the truck, he could see them. All three were still intent on the square.

Carter was halfway to the truck when one of them rolled over the bed and headed for the cab.

His intent was obvious: moving the pickup out and making it a rolling tank.

He saw Carter just as he stepped on the running board. He was toting an M16, but he saw the Killmaster too late to bring it into play.

In mid-stride Carter pumped two from the Luger into his chest. Cloth ripped, blood spread, and the slugs exited, fanning the air behind with flesh.

He had barely toppled out of sight when Nick leaped up onto the hood. His belly hit, and his legs curled. The serrated soles of his boots caught and he was lying belly-out across the roof.

—From *Night of the Warheads*
A New Nick Carter Spy Thriller
From Charter in June

☐ 71539-7	**RETREAT FOR DEATH**	$2.50
☐ 75035-4	**THE SATAN TRAP**	$1.95
☐ 76347-2	**THE SIGN OF THE COBRA**	$2.25
☐ 77413-X	**SOLAR MENACE**	$2.50
☐ 79073-9	**THE STRONTIUM CODE**	$2.50
☐ 79077-1	**THE SUICIDE SEAT**	$2.25
☐ 81025-X	**TIME CLOCK OF DEATH**	$1.75
☐ 82407-2	**TRIPLE CROSS**	$1.95
☐ 82726-8	**TURKISH BLOODBATH**	$2.25
☐ 87192-5	**WAR FROM THE CLOUDS**	$2.25
☐ 01276-0	**THE ALGARVE AFFAIR**	$2.50
☐ 09157-1	**CARIBBEAN COUP**	$2.50
☐ 63424-9	**OPERATION SHARKBITE**	$2.50
☐ 95935-0	**ZERO-HOUR STRIKE FORCE**	$2.50

Available at your local bookstore or return this form to:

 CHARTER BOOKS
Book Mailing Service
P.O. Box 690, Rockville Centre, NY 11571

Please send me the titles checked above. I enclose _____. Include 75¢ for postage and handling if one book is ordered; 25¢ per book for two or more not to exceed $1.75. California, Illinois, New York and Tennessee residents please add sales tax.

NAME_____

ADDRESS_____

CITY_____STATE/ZIP_____

(allow six weeks for delivery.)   A8